Impossibly Small Spaces

In loving memory of Barbara Gene Taylor

Lisa C. Taylor

IMPOSSIBLY SMALL SPACES

Impossibly Small Spaces

is published in 2018 by
ARLEN HOUSE
42 Grange Abbey Road
Baldoyle
Dublin 13
Ireland
Phone: 353 86 8360236
Email: arlenhouse@gmail.com
arlenhouse.blogspot.com

Distributed internationally by
SYRACUSE UNIVERSITY PRESS
621 Skytop Road, Suite 110
Syracuse, NY 13244–5290
Phone: 315–443–5534/Fax: 315–443–5545
Email: supress@syr.edu

978–1–85132–178–0, paperback

Typesetting by Arlen House

Cover images by Russ Taylor

Contents

ACKNOWLEDGEMENTS

Grateful acknowledgement to the editors of the following journals in which some of these stories first appeared, sometimes in earlier forms: *Quail Bell* – 'Second Lives'; *Crannóg* – 'Scientia' and 'Even a Monkey'; *WomenArts Quarterly Journal* – 'Suddenly I Don't'; *The Raven's Perch* – 'Tentacle'; *Tahoma Literary Review* – 'Salt and Blue'; *Flights* – 'Every Body of Water'; *The New Southern Fugitives* – 'Consorts'. 'Salt and Blue' is also an audio recording on the *Tahoma Literary Review* site https://tahomaliteraryreview.com/

Russ, your many hours of support and love mean everything. Thanks to artist Laura Grover for time and art. A shout out to Brendan McNulty for sharing his expertise about vaping.

Gratitude to Claudia McGhee who helped with 'Salt and Blue' and Justin Q. Taylor and Kira D. Taylor for taking time out of their busy lives to comment and edit. To the members of Still River Writers – Charlie Chase, Mary Elizabeth Lang, Garrett Phelan, Claudia McGhee, Suzy Lamson, Jane Katch, Kevin Brodie and David Morse, thank you for listening to and critiquing many of these stories. Thanks to my students, past and present. To my extended community of friends and writers, especially Geraldine Mills, Alan McMonagle, Baron Wormser, Aideen Henry, Ellen Meeropol, John Stanizzi and Lori Desrosiers. To Alan Hayes and Arlen House for your continued support and the writers you champion every day. I'd also like to acknowledge the American Association of University Professors (AAUP) for a travel grant and a faculty development award in 2018 that supported this book.

I am seeking spaces smaller
and smaller: the sooty mouth
of a snake hole, a tree root winding down,
the thin arms of the fungus pushing like
the slow breath of the river.

I have lost the mountains for
mushrooms, their dark winking eyes,
bittersweet taste that holds
a whole season inside.

– Kira D. Taylor, *Morels*

Impossibly Small Spaces

Salt and Blue

The airport monitor indicates George's flight is on time and I think about what I'll say to welcome him home. Love isn't the first word to come to mind, which is, I suppose, progress. A man carrying a bouquet of daisies and a single teal balloon that says *Happy Anniversary* waits next to me. George's letter has been folded and unfolded so many times, the pleats are almost transparent, ink smudged so that some of the words collide, little explosions of 't' and 's', ashy plurals and shadowed singulars.

When the flight status changes from *on time* to *delayed* minutes before arrival, I don't think much of it. Slumped in one of the plastic attached chairs I wait for my phone to charge, tapping my feet in unison with the stranger holding the balloon. When it is done, I detach it from its umbilicus, roll up the plug. The man stares at his phone,

'Oh, God. My fucking God.'

Hunched over and ashen, he shows me the news of Flight 3716. I reach for the powdery paper of my letter while he moans, rocks back and forth, letting the flowers drop, balloon rising to the ceiling.

The man straightens his legs, pushes back thinning hair, while the balloon bobs over us like an inflated lung. His thin mouth pulls in and tears well up, but he sniffles and wipes them away with an elbow. People around us pace and soft chatter accelerates to a din. Perhaps they're wondering who will feed the dog or how much it will cost for the babysitter. Not us. We are crumpled in our chairs, his head now resting in his hands. I check my phone to be sure, praying for a disclaimer, someone's idea of a sick joke. Sports scores and an upcoming local election blare from two television monitors. I conjure the grey door opening, and George walking through, pulling his carry-on with its reliable back-saving wheels.

I match my breath to the stranger with the balloon, a habit I will retain. Without that synchronicity, something else might bubble up in the vast stew of endings and beginnings. What are the odds that the same ending will be served to two different people, strangers waiting for a loved one? He looks at me. My smudged mascara has no doubt transformed my face into a charcoal drawing, some abstract rendition of a woman.

'Are you sure?' I ask.

He shows me an eyewitness view, different from the one I found, this one says something about boats in the area rushing to the scene. Too soon to know about survivors. I hold onto that. Surely there will be a ferry or cruise ship to scoop up the bruised passengers, whisk them to a waiting hospital. I lean in, close enough to smell his Clive Christian.

'Doesn't look good,' he says, choking and swiping at the screen.

We both *know* and that fuses us.

Others start to take notice. Maybe it is my face or his discarded bouquet, the pink cellophane loose and a couple of the daisies already wilting on the carpeted floor. Phones come out of pockets and purses, and a woman with cropped blonde hair holding the hands of two children lets out a wail, starting a chain reaction.

'Daddy, daddy, daddy,' the older child says, each iteration rising in volume.

The man stands up and takes out his wallet and keys and then puts them back as if he suddenly realizes he doesn't need to drive anywhere or buy anything. Finally, an airline representative in a navy blue suit with a red kerchief ushers us into one of those lounges usually reserved for people who pay extra money to board early. He hangs a *Private* sign on the door. Cardboard prints of clouds and jets cover the walls and plush chairs with computer desks line the edges of the room. About thirty of us crowd in and we move like a herd.

'I want answers and I want them now,' a large man in grey sweatpants points his finger almost into the face of the representative. Others hold onto each other, whining children and weeping adults. A spiky-haired older woman rushes forward.

'Are there survivors? I have to know. Are there survivors?' Her face is the colour of molten lava.

'We'll let you know as soon as we have more information,' the representative says.

There is coffee but no one wants to be more awake. Another employee in a dark suit with airline insignia tells us about engine trouble.

'We're doing all we can,' he says. 'We will put you up at the Crestview Airport Suites. More information will be forthcoming in the morning.' Then he apologises as if he'd lost someone's luggage or confused one reservation with that of another.

Three shuttles take us to the hotel and we arrive in the lobby, red-eyed and dishevelled. Counsellors meet us and usher us away from other travellers. We find ourselves in another room with long tables laden with platters of sandwiches and a stack of plates, cups and napkins. No one touches any of it. The woman with children hangs onto another woman and groups of people move in until their arms are around each other, swaying. That's when he finds me and asks if I want tea. We sip from identical paper cups while all around us voices rise, then soften to whimpers and sniffles.

'Our sixth anniversary,' he pulls a small jewellery box out of his jeans pocket and shows me diamond stud earrings.

'Nice.' I didn't know what else to say. What happens to the gifts purchased for lovers who will never return?

'I can't be alone.'

His eyes are bloodshot and his shirt wrinkled as if he's slept in it. I think about those final moments, seatbelts buckled or maybe a flight attendant instructing everyone to brace for impact, the oxygen masks tumbling uselessly from their secret spot above the seats next to the reading lights. George always left the light on, even during night flights. He never could sleep on a plane and would arrive exhausted and grumpy. Closing my eyes, I fast forward through that scene.

The crowd thins as relatives arrive and people lean on fathers and grandmothers, limp off while others look at their room keys and head numbly toward the elevators. We pick the one on the sixth floor, maybe for his six years of marriage.

When we fall onto the bed he reaches for me and, though I know he is closing his eyes so I'll transform into his anniversary woman, I open my legs and arms. The musk of his cologne makes my thighs tremble. A melon-coloured bedspread tumbles to the floor and there are thick terrycloth bathrobes that we wear when we order room service. Later, we share a bath, as hot as we can stand, cleansing and burning at the same time. I mix the bubble bath with shampoo and we luxuriate in foamy steam for more than an hour. Salty tears drop into the tub.

His name is Errol, which rhymes with Carol. Errol and Carol. We don't need last names since he gave his away once and it sank into the sea. After we hear that no one survived the crash, I follow him home.

We have jobs to go to and so we do after a week, telling no one about us, though people send cards, want to bring casseroles and brownies to my condo. I'm no longer there. I tell them I need privacy right now. He explains that his family lives in North Carolina, and they cut off ties when he married Adira. We order takeout until I shop on the weekend while he plans a funeral. Unmarried, I leave the plans to others. No one knows about us, believing I'm with George's family somewhere or perhaps I've gone back to live with my mother and her boyfriend. I don't care what the people in my former life think; they're knitted into the history I left behind.

Adira lives in a teak frame on his mantle; almond-shaped brown eyes and tawny skin. Little dried flowers in front of the picture are scattered like an offering. After a month he turns the photo to face the wall though I know he turns it around when I'm at work, like I reread George's letter and open old emails from him. Our past is in our pores. Where George touched me is where Errol now touches me and maybe after him there will be another, but I don't think so. No one else could taste the salt on my skin and recognise the grief. When George left me I convinced myself that he didn't love Damien the way he loved me even though he told me, softly the first time, then louder.

'I'm sorry, Carol. I love Damien. I love him.'

But the letter promised a meeting swallowed up by the Atlantic, leaving only pieces of wing and fuselage.

Damien emails me, invites me to the memorial service, *A Celebration of George's Life*. What I know is imprinted on my breasts and thighs, in the taste buds on my tongue. I couldn't meet the person who took my place, preferred him to be more myth than man.

Errol borrows my *Atomic Muse* t-shirt to walk by the picture window, morning paper just outside the door. I try the eggs on his plate before sharing my ciabatta. When I lick butter off my fingers I taste old wounds.

'You've over-salted the eggs,' but we understand that it's something else. We've been interchangeable for months now, hoping that each article of clothing or tidbit will bring the clarity or comfort that continues to elude us.

Last night we both slept fitfully, turning over on dreams that seemed to belong to the other. In the morning, he tells me of an elaborate feast set out on Styrofoam plates, bits of foam flecked the *foie gras*; duck *a l'orange* and the towering Pavlova. In my dream, I had scrapes and nicks all over, as if I had been shaving my entire torso with a utility blade. None of the wounds were deep enough to cause anything but superficial bleeding, but they smarted and left rust smears on his eggshell cotton sheets with the absurdly-high thread count. After I awaken, he pushes his way inside of me. Right before he comes, I laugh uncontrollably thinking about his dream and our local restaurant Cleo's serving its *prix fixe* menu on throwaway plates, the snooty maître d' with his waxed moustache and faux French accent waving us away. Errol shushes me, grabs my shoulders, then weeps his way out.

A week after the dream of wounds, I have a dream of skies. I tell him about the vast expanse littered with mountain bluebirds and cardinals, a veritable rainbow darting in and out of clouds. Both of us see cumulous and cirrus and bits of colour. Anyone who has flown knows that clouds cluster, giving passengers a sensation of Heaven. Who hasn't pulled up the plastic shade and looked out the porthole window? Some clouds are blustery old men or wispy schoolgirls and I can part them with my eyes, revealing the bluest truth. We talk about blue because people we love have succumbed to it. We know it's an ending only to us. Our dream-talks become ritual, the night world more compelling than the forward motion of our lives.

After three months we adopt a white cat and call her Cloud. She sleeps in bed with us, mewing and kneading her paws on the duvet. Sometimes I awaken and hear the broken engine of a purr.

His coffee remains untouched on the counter. Today is the day he's chosen to take Adira's clothes to Goodwill. I've moved my clothing into the guestroom closet but keep most of my furniture at my condo because I'm still a visitor here. Everywhere I go in my life from here on out will be temporary. We haul bags into the back of the station wagon; delicate heels in taupe and midnight, silky dresses that drape against the skeleton of a hanger, jeans too small for me. Clothing needs a body and Adira is weightless and body-less. I kiss his lips; touch his naked hand, breathing in the scent that has become my life's fabric and sustenance.

When Damien calls, I am rinsing cups, stacking them in the rubberised metal rungs of the dishwasher.

'I found your number on George's computer,' Damien says. 'I can't go on without him.'

Is it ever possible to forget? I didn't understand why everything shifted and his love became a bee flitting to a more exotic flower, but I did understand Damien's hunger for the small hollow on George's back, the Adam's apple he often nicked while shaving.

When I hang up, it comes to me like the crackle of August heat lightning. The plane crash delivered me here to Adira's husband, loyal, wanting nothing more than a return to months ago when she was stepping out of lingerie, pouring bath salts into their whirlpool tub. I can't fit into her clothes but I have been dabbing her perfume on my wrists and behind my ears, choosing her favourite shades of teal and powder blue, skinny jeans worn with stacked heels. Looking at his clean-shaven face, eyes like moss fringing the road, I feel alive again. He tells me I'm a better cook and he doesn't care that I taste from his plate anymore. He doesn't even mind the dreams I interpret for him and the way I invite him into mine, opening the door as if it were a secret passageway discovered in a house we buy together.

When he returns, we wedge into the crawl space to clear out the remaining evidence of Adira. I find her immigration papers, a wedding album, stacks of scratchy blankets and an infant's christening gown in starched white lace. A patch of light from the window vent flickers and trails over an old trunk like my finger stroking the back of his neck. When he finally lets the door close behind us, a dry heat permeates the room. He sinks into my arms and I hold his weight against me, salt, muscle and bone.

'I can't stop thinking about those last minutes; can't bear to think of her frightened.'

Then he tells me about the ultrasound, how after years of trying she finally conceived three months before the trip.

'We were going to visit her parents, ask her brother to be the godfather. I thought my parents would finally accept her, but my father said he wasn't interested in a half-breed grandchild.'

He chokes on the words as I try to picture this father. My mother would purse her lips when I brought home boyfriends she found unsuitable but my father would grin and stick out his hand, tell us to enjoy ourselves.

'It's wonderful to be young,' he'd say.

The christening gown with its delicate lacework is preserved between sheets of tissue paper in a flat box that we bring downstairs. He's lost two people, one just a sliver of life on an ultrasound. We inhale simultaneously and Cloud rubs up against my leg.

I've thought of George pulling out his phone, trying to call or text in those final minutes, but it's likely there wasn't time and mine wouldn't be the number he'd think of as the plane began its fatal descent.

Errol doesn't seem surprised when I start to load the back of my car with suitcases, my computer and the Vitamix. He helps me carry out my small maple desk. I take one last look at the fireplace with Adira's picture on the mantle still facing the wall, memorise the porch with its two rocking chairs, the stained glass panels on each side of the front door.

'Wait,' he says, and runs upstairs. He returns with the velvet box containing the anniversary diamond earrings.

'For you, Carol,' and he kisses me gently at first, then hard enough for me to feel myself coming back into focus.

Baby Angel

I think about babies, small ones, pudgy ones, pinched-faced ones, babies with smudged cheeks and toothless grins, little tufts of hair tied with pink ribbons, and babies in onesies with an embroidered sailboat or heart on the front. When I have one of my own, I'll love her and keep her close, not like Huck and Rya treat Paradise or what the Jacksons did to me.

When I had been with the Jacksons a little over two years, Mrs Jackson got pregnant.

'It's a sign,' she said. Some useless doctor told her years ago she couldn't have kids. God told them to give a home to a child who needed one, and they picked me. Mr Jackson said I'd be Enid Jackson once they finalised the adoption. I remember everything about the day they took me.

'Look, the one at the table with the green sweater. She's so cute. What is she, seven?' Mrs Jackson wore a mustard coloured suit with high heels like she was going to church. Little Bit was working that day and she told that fancy lady that I was nearly twelve.

'Why is she so small?' Mr Jackson said.

'Don't know, sir. Enid is real smart though. She reads a lot.'

Even though I was almost twelve, no one believed it. Bop said I probably had bad nutrition when I was little. The Jacksons picked me up in an SUV and brought me to their house and I had my own room. I didn't have to share with Rya who stayed at the Village until she ran away with Huck. They have a little girl named Paradise but her life is anything but. Bop said that's another reason why teenagers shouldn't have kids.

'Call me Mom,' Mrs Jackson told me. There was no one called Mom at the Village, no Dad either, just Archie and Gin. On weekends, my favourite staff Dinah and Little Bit worked. Even though she was twenty-two, Little Bit was small like me. She took college classes so she could be a psychologist someday. They made cookies with us and joked around. Children's Village is where a kid has to go if she doesn't have parents or the parents she got aren't fit to raise her.

At the Jackson's house, they had a dishwasher and a linoleum floor. There was a chair where you could put your feet up if you leaned back. The television was bigger than a window and got lots of channels.

'This is your room. I hope you like aqua,' Mrs Jackson said.

I didn't know a colour like a pool or islands in magazines could be a whole room. There was a bed in the middle with a puffy flowered quilt and a teddy bear, even though I was kind of old for stuffed animals. The bookcase had new books, not the kind passed around from kid to kid so the cover was partially off and the pages were all bent or ripped. That first night I read a bunch of them; my favourite was about a girl and her dog that saved a whole family from robbers. When we went shopping, I picked out jeans, striped shirts and a fleece jacket for school. The other girls wore short skirts with leggings so Mrs Jackson bought me some of those too.

'Are you the Jackson's foster kid?' a red-haired girl asked me the first day. I told her I was going to be adopted and we became kind of friends or at least we hung out. Lots of rich kids went to the school and some of them were friendly. Mrs Jackson said I might win a scholarship to college if I made good grades so I tried hard. I kept in touch with kids from the Village even though Mrs Jackson didn't like it.

'You have to move on, Enid. You have a different life now,' she said.

I didn't listen. One thing I know about friends is that a girl needs them. If you find good ones, the kind who let you cry and don't care if you get snot all over the front of their shirt, you'd better hang onto them. Some of them warned me that nothing would be final until the adoption. We were going to court in six months for the preliminary hearing. Then Mr and Mrs Jackson asked me to come into the living room to talk.

'We're going to have a baby. It's a miracle,' Mrs Jackson said. I kind of noticed that she had been looking heavier, especially on top. Mr Jackson smiled at her. My stomach felt like I ate too many tacos, fiery and acidy at the same time.

'You'll have a baby sister or brother,' Mr Jackson said.

I tried to be excited. I could show them how to burp and change a baby. I even knew how to sing lullabies. There were mostly older kids at the Village because babies went to another place to get adopted but sometimes one of the girls had a baby and I'd volunteer to help. Once that child was born, the mother usually left or gave up the baby. I would never give up my baby.

Mrs Jackson gave birth while I was at school, and they named him Gregory, said dumb things like he looked just like Mr Jackson. To me, he looked bald-headed with fat cheeks. I tried to help but Mrs Jackson shooed me away the first time and the second time. They said the baby wasn't my responsibility. Then they started to worry that I might hurt him. I heard them talking.

'She grew up with abuse. What if she tries to smother him or drops him on purpose?' Mr Jackson's deep voice boomed through the wall.

'I know. We don't know what she's thinking,' Mrs Jackson said.

That's the only thing they had right. They didn't know what I was thinking, because if they did they'd know that people at the Village used to call me the baby angel. I'd rock Paradise to sleep before Rya and Huck got into drugs. I even took a babysitting class. I could have told all of that to Mr and Mrs Jackson. Although I lied about some stuff, like breaking their glass elephant and sneaking food, I'd never hurt a baby. At the Village they took away supper as a punishment so I put snacks in my pocket in case the Jacksons might punish me.

'That's disgusting, Enid. Don't you know that you can't have food in your room? It attracts ants and rodents.' Mrs Jackson threw everything out and made me vacuum the whole house and clean the bathrooms. I didn't mind that as much as losing my crackers, peanut butter and apples.

They never left me alone with Gregory and I wasn't even allowed to hold him.

'Can't I hold him? Real gentle?'

'No. He's very young.' Mrs Jackson looked at me with storm cloud eyes, the kind she got when she was barely holding back anger.

'I used to hold babies. Everyone at the Village said I was good at it.'

'Children's Village is not the same as our home. I don't want to hear another word.' Mrs Jackson took Gregory into another room and that night they whispered for a long time when they thought I was asleep.

If Gregory hadn't been colicky, maybe nothing would have happened. I could hear him whimpering from my room so I snuck down the hall and tried rubbing his back. I knew that jiggling a baby worked so I picked him up and moved a little back and forth until he settled down. I had just laid him back in the crib when Mrs Jackson rushed in, her eyes wild. She ran over to check on Gregory even though he was fast asleep.

'Get out,' she hissed. I went back to my room and grabbed that stupid teddy bear. I knew how to curl up so small there was barely a lump in the bed.

They returned me on a Thursday in October, a day when the sun was blinding yellow and the sky clear, with just a few stabs of white. I had a new suitcase filled with clothes and a laptop and I struggled to pull it behind me. I held back tears, at least until the van pulled away. The last thing Mrs Jackson said to me, and it's something I'll never ever forget was, *I know you understand, Enid.* She returned me like a pair of shoes that didn't fit right because I wasn't her flesh and blood. No, I won't ever understand. The Jacksons sent me a birthday card when I turned sixteen but that was the last time I heard from them. Sometimes I hope they wake up screaming like I did for the first few weeks.

I kind of didn't notice Bop before, but when I returned we became more than friends. He stayed up with me a lot of nights, told me it wasn't my fault. Pretty soon Bop and me were kind of a thing and I was glad for it. Later he told me that they didn't deserve me and they'll definitely ruin Gregory. Then he said he'd stick by me no matter what. Bop believed in fate. He had been in the living room reading when I walked through the door. I remember his hair fell over his eye on one side. At first we talked and talked and then he gave me books to read. We'd sneak out of our rooms and meet in the little pantry next to the kitchen after final room check. Because we followed the other rules mostly, no one bothered us. I think the staff felt sorry for me.

'I thought they had already adopted you,' Bop said.

'Pre-adoption. They were close and all but Gregory was their own flesh and blood, as Mrs Jackson said. They didn't know my genes. She said I could have hurt him.' I made a face.

'Yeah. Like we're criminals.' Bop showed his teeth and pretended to look mean but he doesn't have a mean bone in his whole body.

He calls me *Eenie* because I'm not a lot bigger than the kids in middle school though I'm almost nineteen. I call him *Bop*. He dances around even when there's no music because he's got music in his head. I don't always like it.

Bop and me talk about having babies but he said we're not ready and I agree, or concur, as Mr Lightner would say. It's on account of my *abandonment issues*. Now that I'm working, I see Mr Lightner on Saturdays.

Mr Lightner said none of this was my fault and although I know that, I still wonder what I could have done differently. If I hadn't tried to hold Gregory or comfort him or if I didn't hide food behind the books in my headboard, would I be getting ready for college?

'Who is Enid Marie? Do you know her yet?' Mr Lightner asked me last week.

I kind of know what he means because you can lose pieces of yourself when people think a child is like a pet. There are good dogs and bad dogs. Bop never wants a dog on account of the Doberman in his last foster home. He said that dogs only like the real kids, not the invaders. We fight about this sometimes. I miss the Jackson's dog Shondy more than any human. They let her sleep with me. When they gave me back, Shondy got to stay with them. A big poufy dog, she always knew when things weren't right. The day the black van drove up, she whined and whined.

'Shut it, Shondy,' Mr Jackson said. His moustache looked stuck on with glue. Any man that talked mean to a good dog like Shondy should be taken away. Mrs Jackson held Shondy by her collar because she tried to run after the van. She knew what they were doing.

'We're invaders, Eenie. We go in and when the regular kids are there they're the special ones. Even good homes do this,' Bop said.

We left Children's Village when we turned eighteen, Bop's birthday two days after mine. The state gave us money and we found an apartment with a half-sized stove and refrigerator. The rest of the furniture came from the free and recycle store. It only took him two weeks to get a job at The Speed Demon customising fast cars. It took me a lot longer but finally I ended up at the library. Bop thinks I could get a certificate or something so I can be a real librarian.

Bop said the Jacksons will burn in hell for bringing me back to the Village but I know he doesn't believe that any more than I do. Mr Lightner told me that some people let fear run them and decisions made out of fear are never good ones.

'Do you wonder what your birth parents are like?' Bop asked.

'No. You?'

He told me about a dream he had that his parents went to rehab and then came back to claim him. My parents would be in their thirties now. The kids whose parents lost rights had it hardest because we were damaged. One kid had burns on his arm. I only remember being hungry and dragging around a dirty pink blanket.

The last time I saw Paradise, she was screaming her little head off. I bounced her on my hip and danced around the room until she stopped.

'You're real good with babies,' Rya said. 'Want mine? Too much work.'

No kidding, I thought. Gregory Jackson would be four now, maybe in preschool. I wonder if Shondy likes him. I know it wasn't Shondy's fault that the Jacksons were scared. Mr Lightner said some people grow fear bigger in their imagination. They made me into a whole other Enid, one that could hurt a baby. Nothing I said could erase that. I understand that now though I still have a big hole inside of me that Bop tries to fill with songs or peanut butter cookies from the bakery down the street.

Bop and me sometimes visit the maternity ward at Douglas Memorial. Last week we saw a boy who couldn't have been more than fourteen next to a girl in a hospital gown and robe, her belly still swollen. I got close enough to see his pimples and the sweat over his top lip.

'I don't want your fucking help, Darryl,' the girl said.

When she walked away, he looked through the window at the tiny humans in their glass baskets. I guessed one of those babies was his. He stared and stared and I knew Bop was trying to guess whether it was the boy with a full head of curly black hair or the girl with a cap of reddish fuzz. Finally, Darryl put his hands in his pockets and kind of shuffled toward the elevator staring at his sneakers.

I took Bop's hand. Some of the babies squirmed or batted mittened fists but most of them had their eyes closed, dreaming like we dream. Maybe baby dreams are pictures or sounds instead of words. A face. A breast or bottle. A soft touch. The smell of clean laundry. Nothing any of us can count on.

American Tragedy

The man who blocked her path wore a pressed button-down shirt and corduroys paired with boots, the kind that laced up like an old corset. The weather had warmed up after days of cold and Hera's legs begged her to run.

'Please. I don't have anything with me.'

'Whatever. Hand it over.'

'See.' Hera opened her lime green clip-on pack to show her keys, cell phone and meal card.

His open hand slapped her and he dragged her behind a bush like *road kill,* she thought. She scratched and bit his shoulder through his cotton shirt.

'Son-of-a-bitch. Cunt!'

Closing her eyes, she counted to one hundred, then counted backwards by threes. She recalled the details of the schooner last week, Troy getting her sweater out of the backpack, making sure she was hydrated. A clear day, the sky was a curved shoulder of blue above her. Troy took photos of her lounging on the seat in her flowered bathing suit, tipping her sunhat, blowing him a kiss. She put the pictures up on Instagram and all her friends commented how lucky she was to have found someone loving, and smart too.

Floating above the other Hera, the one careless enough to run alone at dusk, she vaguely felt her running shorts being pulled off, pain as her body resisted. Mostly, she concentrated on the boat ride. On their walk after, she balanced on a stone wall and Troy held her hand.

When Robert Morgan Nancy finally released her, Hera pretended to look away while mentally calculating his height, weight and defining characteristics, like the tattoo of a scorpion on his right hand. She lay there for as long as she could to give him a running start. Then she called for help and a white and red ambulance pulled up to the edge of the park. They loaded her onto a stretcher to take her to the Emergency Room where she spent four hours answering questions and having various bodily fluids extracted. The blonde social worker used words like 'brave' and 'blameless' and stressed the importance of prosecution. He was in custody within thirty-six hours.

'It's not something you get over,' Hera told her housemate, Sheena, a week later, drawing the blinds even though it was morning.

'You did everything right,' Sheena said. 'That animal is in prison and can't do this to anyone else.'

'Yeah, I know. It's just that I can't go on as if it never happened.' Hera picked at a mosquito bite scab on her hand until a little spot of blood appeared. Her brown hair was loose, an outbreak of blackheads on her forehead.

'I don't know if I should tell Troy or not. He's coming back for Thanksgiving. I have to go to court in two weeks.'

Every day Hera got up and found a reason why she couldn't go to lectures and readings. People in other parts of the world were walking into crowded marketplaces and blowing up themselves and other people. What kind of a world allowed this? As a scholar focusing on 'Postmodernism in the Contemporary American Tragedy',

Hera had told her advisor that she didn't want a teaching assistantship this semester, citing a need to do more research. She ignored the text messages: *Where r u? How is it going?* An existential dilemma, she thought. Where was she?

Two weeks later, she stopped eating. Her sandwich tasted like wood chips and dirt, a smell she'd never forget.

'You're too thin, lady,' Sheena told her a week after Hera starting living on water and an occasional apple or pear.

'I'm ok. Just not hungry.' Hera straightened the books in the bookcase.

'I read something about this. Could be parasites. I'm taking you to the clinic.'

'Maybe you're right. I keep seeing his face. He's there when I go to sleep. You know, I even smell him, a kind of burnt flesh smell. Makes me nauseous.'

The clinic was on the west side of campus, near the track where Hera ran when she was practicing for a meet. It was the kind of day that used to make her wish fall could last about six months, an edge of ruby on leaves that dotted the trees like an impressionist landscape. Overhead, a gaggle of geese flew in V formation, their cacophony breaking the silence. Sheena squeezed her hand.

Did Contemporary American Tragedies matter? Did literature flatten experience? Writing the word *rape* didn't convey ripped shorts, the burnt flesh smell, fingerprint bruises on her arms. It was a root word for *rapier* and *rapeseed,* words that had nothing to do with the fact that anyone could be violated in countless ways.

The doctor was unnaturally thick like a tree, not fat but solid. When he looked over his glasses at her, she saw pity. Hera watched him scribble on a pile of forms. If she was a bird, she'd be flying south with the migrating geese, letting the wind carry her. She stumbled when she stood up.

Robert Morgan Nancy was the protagonist in The Rape of Hera. *Most readers found him a sympathetic character, beaten by his biological father and molested by his stepfather. His mother never wanted him but had no money for an abortion. She left him in soiled diapers for days sometimes. At age three, he had a hospital admission for dehydration and abscesses on his buttocks. Festering sores. His IQ was in the high average range and he was an avid reader. The only rent he could afford was a third floor walk-up infested with cockroaches and mice. At first, there were minor robberies. Scholars who studied the book concluded that the rape was a minor incident, an attempt at having a modicum of control. This was his first rape. He was on the verge of being evicted from his sixth rental. When Hera had no money, he was overcome by the futility of his situation, said one scholar. She was incidental. The only curiosity was the name of the book, the way the author seemed to point to the rape as a pivotal event when most scholars agreed that it was not.*

Hera concentrated on the cracked yellow paint in the corner of her hospital room. She imagined the fluids from the IV swirling around inside of her, transforming her into a small sea. Sheena brought her a fuchsia plant, magenta and pink flowers dropping like blood spots on the floor. Each blossom had two colours in it, the shade of the inside of a mouth. Tongue and cheek.

The visitor wasn't Troy, but a lookalike. He carried a plastic pot with blossoms like perked-up ears.

'Oh, Hera. Oh, baby.'

The English language is a poor translator of emotion, Hera thought. The Troy-like man put his hand on hers, talked about Thanksgiving, a skiing trip to Aspen that he held out like a winning ticket.

'My father's co-worker will lend us a place. You'll need to get strong though. The black diamond runs are challenging.'

Diamonds came from coal. It made sense for them to be black. Why would anyone wear black diamonds? How to get strong without running? Lie in a bed with a tube of fluid in your arm. Hera nodded; let the Troy pretender peck her cheek, put the ear-plant and a plush blue dog on the table.

'I'll be back tomorrow,' he said.

She nodded again, her fingers playing with the fray of the top sheet.

Books were allowed in prison for prisoners awaiting trial. Ordered directly from a bookstore so it would be certain there was no contraband or sharp objects hidden inside, they would be opened by the guards ahead of time. Robert Morgan Nancy ordered titles by Neil Gaiman and Thomas Hardy. No one talked to him, but the guards took him out for one hour of exercise in a little courtyard once a day. He jogged back and forth across the concrete square for an hour. He had a shower every other day. No visitors.

Hera's parents arrived to collect her on a Tuesday. Most of the furniture had been donated and none of Hera's former clothes fit. Her father threw her duffle bag in the back of the car like a lunch sack. They headed to the rambling cape in Maine with her mother's lily-of-the-valley smell and the quilts her grandmother made on the beds. Her childhood bedroom overlooked her mother's blaze and floribunda roses.

Five hours later, the minor character, Hera, counted the steps it took to walk up the slate path, shuffling a little since the medication made her feel as if she was wading through a viscous substance, her tongue a dead fish. Ice glittered on the rhododendron bush, and the oak in the front yard had claws. Its branches were sprouting muddy worm-like roots, reaching, pulling her down through the depths of the cold ground, a quiet cave with a door hole and hard-packed floor where she could get some rest.

One doctoral student would do a thesis on the ambiguous title and another on the character of Troy, an incidental but startling contrast to Robert Morgan Nancy. Troy had everything, one graduate student said.

Troy visited her in Maine and drank gin and tonics with her father, stayed in the room off the den and left before Hera awakened.

That was only the first visit, argued one scholar. She was more receptive the second time.

'I've made you pancakes,' Hera's father said, 'Blueberry pancakes.'

Hera's mother used to serve them with a side of fresh fruit, a pot of English breakfast tea and a crock of butter. Sunday mornings. Was it Sunday?

Hera took a tentative bite of pancake served on the blue glass plates her mother had picked out. The colour of the sea in August. The melted butter and syrup nestled in the pores of the pancake, perfectly browned. When had her father learned to cook like this? He smiled at her as she cut the pancakes into small squares and drenched each square in syrup.

'I thought we'd go to the point to see the seals. It's not so cold if you dress for it.'

The minor character Hera put on a long-sleeved shirt and a fleece jacket, buckled into the front seat of the Subaru, Mozart on the radio. Grey-dusted clouds muffled the sun. They passed Maynard's Farm Stand, her old elementary school and the houses of friends who moved away years ago.

He pulled into the empty lot. The sun grew stronger and the sand glittered. Hera breathed in the salty smell. The first grey gleaming head surfaced then dove back into the clear water. Soon there were dozens of them looking at her with soulful brown eyes. She pulled off her sneakers and started slowly to walk before her legs told her to go faster, then faster still. One, two, three, four, five, six, seven, eight. Tap, pound, tap, pound, her feet slapped the cold sand.

The seals kept surfacing, brown eyes and wet heads tracking her progress like selkies, seals who shed their skins and became human on land. If a man hid the skin of a female selkie, it would trap her in human form. She would not be able to return to her true form until she found it.

When Hera stopped to catch her breath, her father handed her a water bottle, then pulled her to him, stroking her hair, the brown of a seal's eyes. She tasted the salt of tears before she felt the trickle down her face turn cold on her neck. When she looked back to the sea, a seal close to shore surfaced and its unblinking eyes met hers.

Scholars later conceded that The Rape of Hera *was so titled because Hera proved paramount to Robert Morgan Nancy's fall. Years later a young Ph.D. student would make a correlation between Robert Morgan Nancy's pursuit of learning and Hera's own research. He came to understand, as she did, that literary tragedies define us all. The scholar noted that she was named after the Greek Goddess of love and marriage. Zeus changed himself into a frightened bird so Hera would feel sorry for him. When Zeus turned back into a man, he raped her and she married him out of shame.*

Hera stayed in Maine after the publication of her book, *Breath and Folly: Postmodern American Tragedies Come of Age*, returning only for the trial.

'Were you running alone on the evening of Tuesday 23 October?'

'Yes.'

'What were you wearing on the evening of Tuesday 23 October?'

'Running pants, a long-sleeved shirt and a fleece.'

'Who knew you were on that path?'

'Just my roommate, Sheena.'

The attorney cleared his throat and took a drink of water.

Hera ran her tongue over the back of her teeth, twisted the sleeve of her blouse. Her parents sat in the back next to Troy and Sheena. After two days of deliberations, the jury found Robert Morgan Nancy guilty, sentenced him to fifteen years.

Robert Morgan Nancy would complete his Associate's Degree in prison and publish a chapbook of his poetry.

The seals returned to the point each spring and stayed around until winter, popping up at random intervals during her morning runs.

'They make me feel protected,' she told Troy.

He didn't say anything, just took her gloved hand while she counted the steps to get back to the car.

Suddenly I Don't

My brother Lenny tells me not to give my real name so I call myself Anna, use an old profile picture from Facebook, the one where it's dusk and I'm wearing one of those low-cut sundresses. He'd prefer to set me up with one of his friends but he's already too much in my business. I kind of want to get out there, or at least have a diversion. Gino responded two weeks after my date with the man who blew his nose at the table and four days after the date with Brutus who picked up crumbs with a pre-licked finger and told me about the engine he was rebuilding for a boat he didn't own, though he was sure someday he'd have the money to buy. I'd nearly given up when I spotted Gino's photo.

Nesting phoebes had taken up residence in the little alcove above my back porch, three baby birds. The papa bird dashed back and forth with worms, tiny open mouths clamouring. When I told Lenny, he said I was doing that thing where I romanticise the natural world but it's been a long time since anyone nurtured me. I'd like a bouquet of wildflowers, maybe a home-cooked meal that I didn't have to make myself. The ordinary stuff of dating sites: what was the last book you read? He got high marks for *All the Light We Cannot See* by Anthony Doerr. Gino read poetry, majored in History and English in college. He told me he worked for an internet travel business, managed their website. We decided to wait a month to meet but when he called me I overrode that decision.

'I don't give a damn about your astrological sign or your religion unless you're born again something or pray to a God that tells you to obliterate groups of people.' His voice was deep, almost solemn.

We arranged to meet in a week, in a public place.

I spent at least three days worrying about my appearance although I knew how shallow that made me. What if he found me abhorrent? What if he turned me off? Six years is a long time to be out of a relationship. If Dean hadn't run off with that twit from Cavendish Realty I wouldn't be playing this younger person's game. Well, maybe I would anyway. I should thank him for sparing me the trouble of leaving him.

I talk Hallie into a shopping trip, picked out new khakis and a rose-coloured, lace-trimmed blouse.

'You're worrying too much, Brenna. He's probably nothing like his profile – no one is.'

She should know. She met Olaf on *PlentyOfFish* and Dennis on *OkCupid* but found her husband, Lionel on *JDate* even though she was raised Roman Catholic.

'Didn't want to limit my options. I'd convert for the right man.'

Turned out he didn't care, had only signed up for JDate to please his mother.

'Not religious. You see. Keep an open mind.'

I'd had a hectic day at work and ignored the chirp of a text message on my phone until later.

Something came up. So sorry, Anna.

Who is Anna, a gun-toting, bandanna-wearing gal from the west like Annie Oakley? I wonder if I can return the clothes. I never wear lace-trimmed anything.

When he calls, I fall into the cadence of his low voice, something about his job and a deadline that came out of nowhere. I tell Hallie and she says 'Catfisher' which conjures an image of the whiskered fish and I wonder how that became associated with internet scams. Did he discover my real name and the age of the photo I posted, taken on one of those days when I still believed the good in life outweighed the miserable?

My neighbour's cat killed the papa phoebe. The babies wait in their mud and stick nest, open beaks swallowing air while the cat prowls underneath, hoping for a non-flier to tumble to the ground. Will there be a mother to pick up the slack or am I only assuming the papa was the hunter? No time to grieve. The fledglings will fly or perish trying.

Gino, be truthful with me. Lenny is getting married and I need a date. I'm tired of being the one that everyone whispers about at family gatherings. No one is rushing to fix me up with his or her suddenly divorced brother or widower friend. I'll dance with Gramp who is surprisingly spry at eighty-four. Ma will bring me shrimp and pat my head, making my hair even flatter. Maybe someone will feel sorry for me and I'll get asked to dance. If not, I'll make friends with scallops on toothpicks and miniature quiches, down too many cosmos at the open bar.

'I know you're probably thinking this is bullshit but my job is precarious. The company may be filing for bankruptcy. I'm sorry, Anna.'

I tell him I understand, but I don't. He must eat sometime. Can't we meet later? Outside the sun is blinking on and off. I see my neighbour hoist a huge black bag into the regulation issue trash bin. He's wearing a suit and tie, must have just gotten home. You see, Gino, people have lives after work. My neighbour gets into his Nissan and drives off, maybe to meet a woman or a man, have a dirty or clean martini and some conversation.

'How about Sunday? We could take a walk and go to Shelby's for brunch.'

Good recovery. No one works on Sundays. I guess that means he doesn't go to church. Is it a good idea to let him know that my schedule is wide open? I mean I could clean out my spice cabinet, pay some bills. Hey, I'm on a dating site. It's obvious that I'm available.

'What time?' I ask.

'Let's meet at Sweeny Park at 11:00.'

The khakis and lace won't work. I need a Sunday recreational outfit, something that says leisure without being slovenly. Blue or maybe pink. Walking shoes. Hallie doesn't want to shop again, tells me to just wear jeans and a nice blouse.

'You have those cute sneakers, the ones with flowers on them. Very girly. Denim capris and your linen blazer.'

I think of the afterlife as a school with a uniform requirement. How nice it would be to never again worry about shoes or proper colour matching. Does denim go with pink and is mixing that with flowers over the top?

'Create your own style, Bren. Everyone does it,' Hallie says.

Yeah, everyone on a first name basis with Dior. I don't understand the rules; strive not to commit any fashion misdemeanours. The phoebes have it easy, always smartly dressed in matching feathers.

On Sunday morning I blast Mahler over tea and *The New York Times*. Does Gino read *The New York Times*? No way to know. It wasn't on the questionnaire. I know he is an early riser, likes most kinds of music except opera and country western. A fan of reggae and old jazz as well as classic rock. No deal breakers there. Once married, he has a grown daughter, hates runny eggs, the smell of Citronella and standing in long lines. Impatient and somewhat of a perfectionist is what he said. I told him I'm comfortable with a certain amount of clutter. Not a hoarder. I didn't tell him about the scar, how I could have had reconstructive surgery but opted not to, or that afterward Dean faced the wall at night. I don't know why I didn't choose to have saline-filled pillows on my chest. Flat as a girl now, I only wear the prosthesis when I go out. Hallie says I could still have the surgery. They tattoo nipples on which sounds painful and bizarre. I have imagined myself with pert 34B breasts but I still see the 36C ones I lost. Sometimes I expect to awaken and find them returned like a retriever who sniffs his way home after months away. Do amputees dream their arms and legs restored? I want to be as brave as Angelina Jolie but I don't have kids or a country as my cheerleader.

He's getting out of a grey Prius. I know it's him because he told me he'd be wearing a plaid shirt. Not tall but a respectable height, curly brownish-grey hair. A lot like I imagined, an open and pleasing face with black glasses. Gino. You came for your Anna, free spirit who dances around the house while she whips up Coq au Vin or Teriyaki shrimp over jasmine rice. Anna favours tight jeans and oversized sweaters, reads Mary Oliver and Cheryl Strayed.

Gino heads to Sweeny Park where the rose garden is in full bloom, an obscene barrage of peach, blush red and pink blossoms. I look down at my chest, presentable with the prosthesis. *No one will know*. For a moment I think I'll pull this off until suddenly I don't. I think of another afterlife where our missing parts will find us, maybe in a kiosk where we can check them out like a basketball at the gym, stick them back on where they belong. I imagine a crate of breasts in some corner of my next life and I hope I might not even have a use for them. Maybe breasts will be a body part I'll evolve out of, like baby toes or eyebrows. As I head back to my car, he waves to me. I pretend for a moment that I don't see his wave or notice him walking toward me. This is a new kind of game where a man who may or may not be named Gino meets a woman who is definitely not called Anna. I wish I'd worn the jeans and oversized sweater instead of the capris, but Gino is looking at my face and the roses are peddling their perfume like some violet eye-shadowed woman of a certain age behind the make-up counter at Macy's, and of course the sun picks that moment to shut off, throwing us into the kind of shade that could flatter a corpse.

'So what's your real name?' and I'm telling him how Brenna is after my maternal grandmother, Brenda, who, as far as I know, kept her breasts her whole life though I don't mention the last part because he's smiling at me, telling me he isn't really Gino but Marlon. Like the fish, but not, he says. Brando, of course.

What's the requisite time required to tell someone you're missing breasts? I mean, there's this expectation that body parts are intact, isn't there? There wasn't a place on the questionnaire for this. Are you missing a leg, testicle, breast or an internal organ? Are you still in treatment for said missing part? Is that your real hair or a wig? I decide to wait until after brunch. The roses are pushing me to be optimistic with their petals and healthy stalks. An adult phoebe flies by and I'm wishing it was a mouse and not the papa phoebe eviscerated by the cat.

I slip it in before the second cappuccino.

'Are you well now?'

'Yeah. I mean I'm fine. Except for. You know.'

He sips his coffee as if I just told him I'd once kept an overdue library book without paying the fine.

'Thanks for telling me.'

I nod in the way people do when they aren't exactly sure what other response might be required. Do you want to know about any of my other deformities? I have a root canal and my little finger is crooked from the time my brother Lenny bent it back and it was in a splint for a week. I don't actually think I look that bad without breasts. This is the body I've been given, for better or worse. I suppose it could always be worse as my mother used to say. Or better, as Dean would have said if he hadn't decided that this was way more than he bargained for when he said *I do*. I'm not blind or deaf. I can pretty much do anything I used to do and I even look decent in one of those special bathing suits with the built-in prosthesis bra.

Marlon has moved on to talking about a book he's reading, tells me how beautiful it is, this book, and his face looks less angled and more rounded. I like his nerdy glasses and the way he curls his stubby fingers around the yellow ceramic mug.

I thought I'd gotten pretty good at the minimalist dating game: dinner, dancing, drinks, until I developed a migraine or felt queasy or I forgot that my sister/cousin/best friend was arriving early tomorrow from Greece or Panama. With Marlon I order some fresh-squeezed orange juice that the server calls *incredible*. He may soon walk past those lewd roses and drive home to log onto the dating site. Suddenly I don't care.

'My brother is getting married next month. Want to go to a wedding?'

Marlon looks at me, blue eyes flecked with grey.

'Will there be shrimp and little quiches?'

'No doubt. I'm expecting a Forrest Gump extravaganza of shrimp.'

'Cocktail, scampi, stuffed?'

'Gumbo, teriyaki, kebabs.'

'I hate shrimp. Bottom feeders. But I'm a sucker for those tiny quiches, like an abbreviated breakfast food.' He declines a refill on the coffee from the attentive waiter, puts a credit card on the check and won't consider splitting it.

When we head outside I smell the roses before we see them. Marlon tells me he has to work on some website and all I can think of is his questionnaire and what he'd change about it. Then Lenny texts me; he's heading to the Farmers' Market with Sheila and do I want to meet? I tell Marlon I have to go.

'Boyfriend?'

I give Marlon what I hope is an aloof look and he kisses me on the cheek.

'I'll call you ... or you can call me.'

When I inform Lenny that I have a date for the wedding, he looks a little too pleased, but Lenny has one of those faces that always seem frozen in a half-smile.

'Anyone I know?'

'No. Man I met online.'

Sheila exchanges a look with Lenny. Those two are about as subtle as Fox News. Maybe my comeback won't be with Marlon of the deep voice and blue-grey eyes. They change the subject to the DJ they've hired, a friend of Lenny's. Isn't it interesting that an orthopaedic doctor would want to moonlight as a DJ? I handle the bell peppers and treat myself to a loaf of artisan bread.

My attendant's dress is form fitting but no one who doesn't already know can tell. The wonder of fake boobs. When we dance, his hand lingers at my waist and I don't want the music to stop even though it's 'The Power of Love' and I hate that song. He's an adequate dancer, only steps on my feet once. I'm wearing dyed silk green heels that I'll throw out after the wedding.

'I ate at least eight of those mini quiches. Abundant quiche. Abundant shrimp.' He's whispering and I can smell the alcohol on his breath. We've already toasted Lenny and Sheila at least twelve times, watched them dance as if this was their first wedding and we're all twenty-eight or thirty again. Lenny says sometimes it takes a lot of tries to get it right.

'I only came for the food,' I tell Marlon before he vanishes. He's mysteriously absent for the cutting of the cake, the bouquet tossing, Lenny and Sheila taking off in a limo for their honeymoon in Maui. Gramp and I dance the final dance and he tells me that green is a good colour on me.

'Reminds me of a Douglas fir.'

When he spins me I almost fall off the stupid heels before I recover my balance, dip and spin again to the music of yet another love song, catching a glimpse of Marlon only at our splashy finish where I curtsy and Gramp bows, doing a courtly flourish with his hands. Marlon has taken off his tie and jacket and unbuttoned his top button. He leans against the far wall next to a fake potted plant, car keys dangling from his hand as he scans the thinning crowd. When he spots me, he raises one finger and I think what the hell is that supposed to mean? It's not a V for victory or a peace sign and it's not *the finger* brush-off. I wonder if I missed the lesson in dating cues. He does it again so I kiss Gramp and make my way to the wall.

'Needed some breathing room,' he offers as an explanation for his hours long absence.

'You missed the Macarena and YMCA.'

'I guess I'll have to find a way to live with myself. You know your shoes are molting.' He points to a spot on the instep of my left foot where green has stained my nylons.

'Yeah. Disposable. I buy new ones every week.'

Marlon takes my elbow and whispers: 'I've got a secret desire to get on a plane to Maui so we can interrupt their honeymoon. They're too old to do this unsupervised, don't you think?'

'I'm in if you're in. Just let me call work and tell them I'll be taking advantage of their instant vacation programme.'

'Am I being too forward to suggest you should change your clothes? A gown will weigh you down in the water,' Marlon says.

'I'll consider it.'

I open the door to his Prius and find a cappuccino waiting in the cup holder, *Anna* scrawled in magic marker on the Starbucks cup. His laptop case is on the back seat next to an overnight bag.

'Are we going somewhere?'

'I've had enough caffeine to drive through the night. How about you?'

Marlon-Gino, I don't even know you. Maybe Lenny and Sheila know you and maybe they don't. Those two exchange looks that seem like code but I could be reading into it. My mother's face looms above me. *Brenna, this man is a stranger. That's why a woman should always bring her own car on a date.* This from a woman who married at nineteen after meeting my father at a flea market.

'I'm thinking ocean. Maybe it's the colour of your dress or the moon. Let's stop and pick up some clothes for you.'

I never told Marlon where I live. Dating site 101. Meet in a public place. Continue to meet in public places until you're sure. We've had five dates, all in restaurants. Yeah, we've taken walks and watched a sunset together once.

The banquet hall parking lot is emptying out.

I sip Anna's cappuccino. Sweet, the way I like it.

It's Friday night or nearly Saturday morning. I'm about to go somewhere.

'Where were you?'

Marlon takes off his glasses, rubs his eyes.

'I feel like an asshole for telling you this. Remember when you told me about your cancer? I figured we'd just be friends and I wouldn't have to deal with it but then, well, something happened.'

'What do you mean?'

'Let me finish before I lose my nerve. I was afraid I'd be turned off by, you know. So I left, went to the all-night place on Spruce and Prospect, drank a whole lot of coffee. I don't want to be the kind of man who sees women as breasts or ass, but shit, I'm no saint. I was going to send you a note and explain that this isn't a good time for me to be in a relationship, etc, etc. An old guy was sitting on one of the stools so I bought him an early breakfast. He told me his wife died two years ago and he's never gotten over it. He cried.'

'I'm not dying, Marlon.'

'I know. So I left the wedding, thinking I wouldn't come back. Didn't want to lead you on and I didn't want to deal with sex. What if I can't perform? You deserve better. But I hated myself for it. Not the kind of man I want to be. So we're going to the ocean tonight and we're going to face this thing. I'll understand if you don't want to go but I want this more than a better job or even miniature quiches.'

I tell him about the phoebes, how it isn't fair that one species can exploit another and that sometimes even when I want to, I can't protect those who need it most. He nods and hands me a bag with sunscreen and a pair of rhinestone-studded sunglasses.

'I don't have a cat,' he says. 'We won't get one, ok?'

So we stop at my place and I pack the special bathing suit, my best cover-everything nightgown and a book. How can I hate a man who just admitted to being an asshole? That's the part Dean never got, that it was ok to feel uncertain, angry and even turned off. It just wasn't ok to leave me because of it. I'm still the same Brenna and I guess that's why I didn't opt for reconstructive surgery. A part of me wanted to make peace with this change and a part of me revelled in the fact that it didn't kill me.

He had booked us into a hotel in Dennisport as Gino and Anna Virello.

'Breakfast is served from eight-thirty to ten, Mr and Mrs Virello.'

'Ah, Gino Virello. You're definitely the man for me,' I tell him as we ride the elevator to the fourth floor.

He opens the sliders and tangy air fills the room. I take in the king-sized bed, chocolates on the pillow.

'Nice touch, Mr Virello.'

He whispers something I can't quite hear.

'Think about floating,' I tell him. I'm cold, maybe from the early morning air or something else. If I had nipples they'd be hard. I think of those nipple tattoos, how they can't do anything real nipples do. Marlon starts to undress and it's my turn to unbutton my shirt, shed the cotton camisole I wear sometimes instead of a bra. I start with the bottom buttons, my hands struggling to push the button through. He takes over, kissing every inch of exposed skin until he runs his fingers over the ridges where my breasts used to be, bends his mouth to the scars before he moves up to my lips. By the time we tumble onto the huge bed, the sun is climbing higher, pinpoints of light on the ceiling and walls.

'We're going to miss breakfast, Mrs Virello. What about those little quiches?'

'Sometimes you just have to go without,' I say before drifting off to the sound of the Atlantic shushing the noisy gulls.

Even a Monkey

When he whacked the top of the clock to stun the Zen flute music into silence, I was in a half-sleep, the kind where covers felt like swaddling and the breeze made me shiver like my first crush.

'Don't forget your meeting with Jessup.'

Thomas is my timekeeper, punctual to a fault while I meander through my ablutions, nicking myself with the too-dull razor, noticing a line of shaving cream still on my face. I hate shaving because it's a ritual. Only when we are on vacation do I let the shadow on my face roughen until Thomas runs his hand over it with his smooth fingers, fingernails clipped and clean.

'You need a shave, man.'

I didn't mind placating him. In exchange, I get to live in a townhouse with a king-sized bed and velvet draperies, maid service and antique furniture. Weekend getaways to the mountains or seaside are important to Thomas, and I enjoy those times as well. He asks little of me other than I keep clean, faithful and practice good dental hygiene.

'Have you ever thought of modelling, Lee?'

I pull my face into an unassuming pose.

'Nah. I would hate everyone looking at me.'

I know he's smiling because he relishes having me all to himself. It's part of the story he's built, that I am unaware of my looks. If I could sell the names of men who have told me that, I'd retire.

Pops took us out of Boston years ago and we never again lived in one place. I got a taste for awakening to prints of cardboard sunsets on motel walls and exit signs on the highway. I'd ride up front with him while Sadie worried the upholstery in the back.

'Where we goin' Pop-Pop?'

'Ah, Sadie-sugar, we're on an adventure. Gonna see the big world. Don't you want your Pop to have opportunity?'

Sadie didn't answer. We both knew that we would be packing up in a few months because of missing money or Pop's fight with a co-worker. At nine, I had to change schools because Pop called my teacher a frigid bitch. *A man needs to stand his ground, son,* he'd say. Not me.

Thomas pushes me out the door but not before he kisses me twice, fills my travel cup with my favourite pour over Mexican single origin and hands me a homemade lemon poppy seed muffin. He tells me I look like Ryan Reynolds, recently voted *People* magazine's Sexiest Man of the Year. I return his kisses, feel his gym-toned biceps. I know that he's trying to make me into a better person. Under his tutelage I can now choose a good wine and order with a respectable accent at a French restaurant.

'You'll do fine, Lee. Just be yourself.'

Bad idea. Prospective employers want to see the image of what they think they're looking for. My job is to convince them that I am a lab assistant. I'm not a good worker, being lazy and forgetful by nature. But Thomas believes in me and since we've only been a couple for eight months, I don't correct this overestimation of my skills.

Pops called last week from La Connor, Washington.

'Got a job as a bartender in this trendy bar with licence plates from all over on the walls. You should visit. The writer Tom Robbins lives here. Didn't he write some crazy shit?'

Yeah. Shit about a hitchhiking woman with a huge thumb. Used to read his books after I took whatever chemical concoction was offered. Most of the towns Pop chooses have one bar, one diner; men in stained polyester shirts perched on bar stools drinking cheap see-through beer.

I sip from my travel mug and bite into a muffin that isn't the slightest bit dry. How does he do that? Thomas is great. My last boyfriend had this tattoo addiction. I didn't know that was a thing until Miles. Apparently, one or three isn't enough and these people want every inch of their body covered with snakes or Chinese symbols. I couldn't get past the red and blue skin. It looked less like art and more like a disease. But Thomas is unblemished, just trots off to the law firm in a Calvin Klein suit with a grey silk tie. Still, it's time I pushed off. I hate to overstay my welcome, have him bitching about Jessup and how a monkey could have gotten the job he set up. Even a monkey has his limits.

I drop my tie and cell phone in the bin by the train station; buy myself a ticket to Anacortes, Washington. Usually I stay about ten days, just long enough to go to the library and look up the next place I might want to be: Port Townsend, Washington or Eugene, Oregon. Thomas' idea to have the joint account, a way to trust each other. I'll miss his clean smell and how servers ran around trying to please him. If Thomas hadn't pushed me to get a job, I might still be strength training at the gym, or driving his Mazda down the strip. Instead I'm sipping watery coffee from a paper cup in a train station.

No way to tell Thomas that a year and half at a community college didn't make me a lab assistant. See what happens when you trust a monkey? Monkeys steal, even from their pops. That's why he locks up his cash and prescriptions. I'm welcome to eat his food and crash on his couch until I find a place to begin again.

The two good suits and five designer shirts in my duffle will be key to my new story – burned out hedge fund manager or CEO of a start-up bought out by one of those big conglomerates.

I'll be looking for a man in Levis and Tony Lama boots, a man who isn't afraid to get his hands dirty.

TENTACLE

I dreamed I gave birth to a baby with a tentacle, awakened with sheets damp and clinging to my rotund belly. When a single woman of a certain age is pregnant, bad dreams are the least of it. Yesterday, I snapped at the server in my favourite diner. She had bluish circles under her eyes and her hair was tied up with what looked like a shoelace. After she looked down at her regulation white shoes, I told her about the tentacle. Nothing like a good story to alter the energy in the room.

I pray to no one in particular that all of my baby's limbs and organs will be normal. Even though I wasn't sure about the pregnancy for the first three months, I've been good ever since.

I awaken to the sound of Joel knocking at my door. He has a habit of waking me up and I know it's because he worries. I'm the little sister gone wrong.

'Get up, Brooke.'

'Ok. Hold on.' I pull my bathrobe around the ratty *Disturb the Universe* t-shirt and panties I'm wearing. Saturday. Why bother getting dressed? Pregnancy isn't a fashion statement and I've been minimalist in the maternity attire purchases. Joel loans me t-shirts.

My brother pushes his way in and plunks an ominous looking juice beverage on the counter between the kitchen and the rest of the room. He's taken to going to LifeJuice on the weekends and he is convinced that juice will save me. Last week it was carrot-kelp-ginger-turmeric. I poured the rest down the sink when he left. I tentatively sip at this one and it's pretty good.

'What is it?'

'Berry-carrot-banana.'

That actually sounds like food. I drink some more and Joel's face crinkles into a smile.

'Thatta girl,' he says and I feel like the first horse in a race, probably a good metaphor for a pregnant lady.

Joel kind of half-sits and half-leans on one of my stools. He's tall so he can stand-sit, his butt only slightly inclined toward the flat part.

'I found you a bigger place,' he says, the smile spreading wider.

'But this is compact. Easy to clean.'

My apartment is modest by modest standards. The landlord calls it an efficiency, which is landlord-speak for one room. There isn't much efficient about one room unless a person enjoys having breakfast in bed. The bathroom is small enough for the door to hit the sink when open. Even so, the rent is breaking me, though I've made plans I'll set in motion once octopus baby arrives.

That's when he tells me about the house he bought, how we'll share it, four bedrooms and a backyard. Joel is a physician's assistant and makes good money. I had to switch to part-time in my job as a physical therapist because I couldn't lift, and standing all day made varicose veins pop out on my legs.

I'm not sure how I feel about living with my brother. He's a good man, even though he has terrible taste in women, his marriage a catastrophe. I don't know if he even dates anymore. Those kinds of questions are off limits, which is why he's never asked me about the father of my little octopus. My favourite game is to pretend she doesn't actually have a father because the four times I slept with Pierre were that surreal. Each morning, he would disappear before I awakened, no note, no coffee on the counter. Ghost lover. After the fourth time, he left behind a gorgeous paisley tie. His cell phone went to voicemail each time I tried him. Timing is an art form. Finally he left a message, but like most things related to Pierre it was noncommittal. He said he'd swing by to pick up the tie.

Sometimes I think about Pierre returning, but there isn't a single scenario that seems workable. He just shows up one day to get his tie and we resume our sex-centred relationship, only now a baby with a tentacle is vying for his attention. She can stretch the tentacle across the room, muss his hair and slap his olive-complexioned face. He'd call her bébé, brush her tentacle away like a housefly. *I should have known that a girl like you would give birth to a mollusk.* I'd throw the tie at him and tell him to get out. After all, he just called my baby a mollusk. Who needs a man like that?

'You're not responsible for me,' I tell Joel. By now I've sucked down the juice beverage and I can feel the vitamins fortifying both of us. She is doing flip-flops and then gets the hiccups. It's the oddest sensation having the body inside my body have a bodily function I can feel. I like it a lot.

'Don't start. You think I don't know that? Look. I have the money and I want to help. Besides it will be fun raising my niece. I'm not so good at marriage but I'm great with children.'

'Perfect online dating profile. Lots of takers.'

'Seriously, Brooke.'

It isn't possible for me to be serious, especially about this. Besides pregnancy is absurd. It makes me waddle.

I duck into the bathroom to change my clothes. I keep them in the miniature chest there because efficiency doesn't mean privacy even though they both end with 'cy'. The doorbell rings. Who would drop by on a Saturday morning? Did I get a package? Maybe it is a darling layette for my baby cephalopod. Then I hear low voices. Men, definitely men. Has Joel arranged a marriage for me to save my honour?

'Meet your husband, Brooke. I've chosen him from a pool of twenty applicants who want to marry a pregnant woman. He has good teeth and a steady income.'

I brush my teeth. It is never a good idea to meet ones' prospective mate with bad breath. When I crack the door, Pierre is chatting it up with my brother as if six months was simply an oversight.

'Oh, *merde*! I forgot to call for one hundred and eighty-five days. My bad. And what about that tie – the one with the swirls that look like sperm?'

When I make my grand entrance, and it is definitely a grand entrance, Pierre's perfect skin is dancing around blotchiness and his eyes are riveted on my swollen belly. God, this bebé will be gorgeous if she takes after him. It's not like I'm hideous but he is right out of *The New York Times* fashion section. He doesn't comb his hair, he tousles it and lets it fall perfectly over his unlined forehead.

'Who is the lucky man?' Pierre moves forward in that distinctive way of his, half dancer and half gigolo.

'You,' I say. 'Welcome back, Daddy.'

Joel looks like he's about to trip over his own humongous feet. I guess it's hard to think of your sister doing some dude, even one as breathtaking as Pierre. Yes,

Joel. Women are that shallow. Pierre's eyes close nearly to slits as if contemplating his next move. It's not often that I render men speechless.

'How do you know?' he finally asks.

'Hmmm. I'm guessing based on the fact that you are the only possible candidate.' I straighten my back, which pushes my belly out even more. My hair isn't even combed and it is my best feature.

'By the way, where the hell were you? I mean, things seemed to be going ok and then you disappeared altogether instead of just sneaking out in the early hours.' I finger comb my waves and stare at him without blinking.

'Business trip.'

He states this as if being out of touch for half a year is a normal way for adults to conduct relationships.

'No worries. I wasn't expecting to marry you. The vanishing act doesn't work for me. This wasn't planned but here I am and here she is.' With my hands on my belly, I look like Buddha.

'A girl?'

'Yes. Joel here bought a house. We're going to raise her. You can kick in child support and get on with the serial dating,' I say, mentally calculating the dimensions of the sandbox I want to build.

He looks both angry and relieved. Only Pierre could do this with so little affect. I'm sure he'll want DNA testing and he'll probably find a good lawyer to make him look less rich.

'Monique, that's what I'm going to call her.'

Pierre frowns and he is doing the slit-eyed thing again. Hard to dismiss a baby with a name. Monique kicks me. I think she is trying to get her father's attention. To his credit, he gives me a new phone number and pecks me on the cheek. I hand him the tie.

'Complete asshat,' Joel says when we hear his car pull away. 'But hot, very hot.'

Pretty strange to have my brother rate a guy I had casual sex with, even if it did result in a pregnancy.

'Yeah. Monique is a lucky girl.'

He has no idea.

Joel promises to call and bring me to see the house tomorrow night. Not a bad guy, my brother, even if his taste in juice and women are questionable.

By the time I went into labour on a July night, we had already closed on the house and I had obtained the best lawyer in town. I only want Monique to have everything she needs and I knew Pierre would hate his wife in Lyon to find out how he spent his time in the States. It only took two visits to The Colony Club to find him: smart, fit and a face like a young Johnny Depp. The tan line on his left ring finger gave it away. By the time I had sidled up, he had noticed me as well. That Stella McCartney colour block dress from the secondhand shop did the trick.

No one thought to tell me that this hurts. The classes were all about breathing and having a supportive coach, like those were the only things I'd have to worry about. I visualize Monique slipping out like the little mollusk she is, but the suction cups of her tentacle keep catching. I scream *merde* until finally it is over. The pain stops as abruptly as a plane touches down on a runway. We have arrived at our final destination. A nurse hands me a white blanket-wrapped bundle. Black hair, teeny nose and heartbreaker eyes. I unwrap her slowly until two perfect hands flail at me. No tentacle though I suspect now that one might appear to reel me back in whenever I try to venture away from responsibility.

Monique looks at me through her long lashes and her tiny fist closes around my finger. The white walls, stainless steel cart and juice with a bent straw disappear. She blinks as if she'd just arrived in a foreign city and I want to say, I understand. I don't know anything about this landscape and will have to rely on nonverbal communication and generous financial support for now.

Snug in the crook of my arm, head warm against my swollen breast, I stroke the spot on her head where the bones have not yet fused, feel a warm rush at the sight of her snail hands. Somewhere, far away, my phone dances on the table. Closing my eyes, I float with Monique out of her sea home to a garden with irises and zinnias, a wicker-backed rocking chair and zero juice beverages.

Every Body of Water

Brett described the acrid odour that lingered on him for days after the fire, bits of photo albums and picture books that swirled in the November wind. Of course, she wanted to see where he grew up but he said his hometown had virtually shut down after the paper mill closed. Anyone who could get out moved to the city and those who were too old or scared of change made the best of it bagging groceries or working in municipal services.

'We moved to Cedarville after that,' Brett said, telling her about the ride back to the shell of their house where he saw one of his Converse sneakers on its side, the rubber blackened and shoelaces frizzled like string potatoes sometimes served on the top of salads at the Green Goddess. The visit to a comma of sand they called a beach at the end of the next road only made him think of what he'd never again have. Tanaya laid her head on his shoulder.

'Poor thing. What happened to your mother?'

'Never recovered, blamed herself. She's a smoker. We stayed at a Quality Inn for three weeks, then an apartment.

Ma didn't have any family and Pa's folks lived in Tennessee.' He added in the part about Tennessee because of Nashville. In his mind, he saw a woman with platinum hair and a guitar slung over a muscular shoulder singing from the back of a pick-up truck.

'Sucks that you had to go through that.'

She had moved closer to him on the couch and he smelled her perfume, lemony and floral at the same time. Her sweater was the colour of tropical fish, an Electric Blue Johanni like the one his boss Otis had in the tank between his kitchen and dining room. Otis had a special shelf built so the tank could be visible from both sides. *Manny,* he called that shimmy of blue. Did Manny have the consciousness to know he was in a prison or did every body of water feel the same?

'You should get a fish tank, Brett. Best way to attract the right kind of ladies.' They were smoking a blunt at his house after tax season finally ended. Otis once had a wife, or so he said. Brett didn't want a fish tank though it was entertaining to watch Manny swim in and out of faux coral reefs, especially when he was high.

'Once we found blackberries growing wild. My father was scared. What if they were poisonous? I showed him the picture on Wikipedia but he still didn't believe me,' Tanaya sipped her tea and sopped up the tiny spill on the saucer with a napkin. 'I ate a whole handful but he couldn't believe you could get something safe for free.'

'Did he finally try them?'

'No. I guess if you're afraid of something, it isn't easy to get over it,' she said.

'I used to be afraid that my mother would fall asleep with a lit cigarette and start another fire,' Brett said.

'Is that why you hate campfires?'

Last summer their friends had a fire on the beach. Tanaya was pumped about s'mores and roasting hotdogs on sticks. She had purchased fireworks and planned to shoot them off at midnight. He only showed up to watch the sunrise. Fireworks sounded too much like death.

When he married Tanaya, they'd have two kids. The first one would be a boy and they'd name him Nathan. Tanaya wanted a girl named Katrina but that reminded him of New Orleans and the levee. Never name kids after a disaster. Tanaya grew up with hand-me down clothes so it would be Brett's job to make sure she and their kids were well dressed.

'When am I going to meet your mother?' She snuggled up to him.

'Ma's kind of shy.'

He could use a blunt right now. They left with Ma on a Wednesday. He had walked to the beach one last time. Low tide and already hot. Horseshoe crabs got stuck and he wasn't sure they could dig their way out so he picked up a few and threw them back in the water. Once Ma packed up the van, she told them to get in and they took off. Bella was ten and Brett was twelve.

Truth was he didn't know what his mother would think of Tanaya. He didn't know what she thought about anything since the suicide. Brett never thought of his mother as beautiful but most men did, tall men, paunchy men, nerdy men with glasses. They all wanted to take her out to the movies or to dinner and a hotel. She'd dress in a tight black or red dress and high heels.

'You kids be good now. Pizza money on the counter.'

Got so Dominos knew their order as soon as they picked up the phone. He kept calendars so he could cross off the days until he could legally leave. Poor Bella. Brett applied to colleges far away, ended up at the University of Massachusetts. Then the call came in about Pa.

Tanaya pulled on his sleeve, pouted, her brown-black hair tied back in a ponytail. She wore low jeans with a wide leather belt. He wanted to kiss her. He always wanted to kiss her.

He didn't know why he made up the story about the fire; maybe to burn up the memories of all the nights where his mother would call to say she wouldn't be coming home. He dreamed of a colonial house with a fireplace where they'd hang their stockings on Christmas Eve, leave cookies on a plate for Santa. Instead they got extra money on Christmas so they could order an everything pizza from the one sorry place that was open. Just Brett and Bella while Pa had a life sixty miles away that they didn't know anything about until he blew his brains out one New Year's Day. When they went to clean out his apartment, they found stacks of comic books, a collection of GI Joes, and no clues except a letter to Ma that she wouldn't share. By then only a year was left on the calendar, and Bella had become Ben.

Ma asked him what he did for work the last time they talked.

'I do people's taxes.'

'Do you need college for that?'

He heard her coughing. Emphysema or COPD. That part was true. She smoked as long as Brett could remember. She once told him she liked the look of it. High heels, tight dresses and a cigarette. Kind of a uniform.

Brett would kill her off soon. Car accident. Lung cancer. No matter how he spun it, she wouldn't be possible in his story. Though she had aged, she still favoured sheath dresses and heels, always had a middle-aged man on her arm. His Ma was a genius at making loser men feel wanted. She just didn't use the same skills with her kids. Bella told him about the boy inside of her, her true self, and Brett understood. Now Ben was training to be a nurse-midwife and had a girlfriend. Brett filled him in on Tanaya.

'Good for you, dude. Let the past blow the fuck away,' Ben said.

Tanaya was the beach Brett landed on. Nothing could be salvaged from the past except empty pizza boxes and calendars with days crossed off. When Tanaya found a photo of Ma, short body-hugging dress and cigarette held just so, he had already told her about the fast-moving metastasis that would consume his mother before they'd have a chance to meet.

At the corner pub, Ben's hazel eyes and long eyelashes garnered looks from the women.

'Can I meet your lady?' he asked.

'Sure. Come for dinner. Tanaya makes this dish with green chilies,' Brett said, wiping beads of liquid off his glass.

They invented Little League games with Ma cheering them on, handmade Christmas stockings with their names embroidered in gold thread and a plate of cookies for Santa with a few bites taken out of each on Christmas morning.

Brett told him about the fire.

'Perfect, man. Burn it up – the whoring, the goddamn pizza. A fucking pyre.'

'I told Tanaya that Pa taught us to ride bicycles, starting with those training wheels,' Brett said.

'Whatever you say, bro. Didn't learn until I was eighteen, right before the surgery. Why do you think he had all those GI Joes?' Ben asked.

'Ma said he couldn't pass the physical because of his eyesight. Maybe he wanted to be a soldier.'

'Scary to think of him in a war zone. Wouldn't have lasted long with that temper,' Ben said. 'Strange how we never really got to know him.'

They agreed on a date for the dinner.

Tanaya fussed about the menu, insisted on cloth napkins and a tablecloth. She put out the silver candlesticks and placed a single yellow rose in a bud vase.

'Can't wait to meet your brother. He taught you stuff, right?'

'Kind of the other way around. Ben is younger,' Brett said.

'Is he ok with spices?' Tanaya crunched up cilantro and added it to the pot.

'He loves spicy food.'

'Does he drink?'

Brett laughed. 'Ben holds his liquor better than anyone I know.'

When the doorbell rang, Tanaya tucked an errant hair into her ponytail, her flowered dress covered by an apron that she rolled into a ball and hid behind her back.

'Hey, man,' Brett said, pulling his brother into a hug. Ben only came up to his neck.

Ben handed them a bottle of Pinot Noir.

'This must be the lovely Tanaya.'

By dessert, they hit their stride; Ben's finger caught in a car door and Ma's panic on the way to the emergency room, Brett's winning science fair project and all the photos Ma took that burned in the fire. Brett really did win the science fair but only Bella and his classmates attended the assembly. Ben told her about the nurse midwife programme.

'Women don't mind a male midwife?'

'More common than you think,' he said.

They looked at each other and Brett clicked his spoon against the empty custard dish.

'How did your father die?' Tanaya asked.

They both startled and he let Ben have this one.

'Car accident during an ice storm,' he said. 'He skidded.'

'Right off an embankment.' Brett added. 'Between that and the fire, our mother never recovered.'

'How could she?' Tanaya started clearing the dishes.

'Coffee or tea?' she called from the kitchen.

They could hear her grinding coffee, rinsing plates.

'You did well, big bro. Beautiful lady.' Ben said. 'What are you going to do the next time Ma calls?'

'Oh, she won't be calling,' Brett said. 'I changed my number.'

Natural Causes

Everyone dies, but not like this. *Unnatural,* they told her daughter, Hannah, after her mother Sonya's pocked and grey body was lifted into the back of the ambulance. Her mother had kept the log cabin spotless, even dusting the rough-hewn walls and beams daily. Her mother's friend Mira visited often, staying for weeks at a time. No one knew where Mira lived the rest of the time; only that she drove a vintage Ford pickup truck. Clues included Sonya's stocked medicine chest, a pile of unfinished letters and a computer that looked as if it had been ravaged. It would be weeks before the autopsy results came in.

'I couldn't look at the body. Jeez. I mean I wouldn't do it. I told them I'd turn my back if they tried to make me, focus on the wall or my hands or something.' Hannah hugged her voluminous leather bag, raked her fingers through short hair.

'Remember the storm when we visited last summer? Screen door banging like something out of a horror movie. Mom's phone was ringing and ringing, almost hopping off of the kitchen table. She wouldn't answer it, kept pacing. This place creeped me out.' Hannah blew her nose on a

Kleenex she pulled out of her bag. Her husband, Lex, reached a hand to touch her on the shoulder but she pivoted. 'Used to pretend I was adopted by a family like the Strands next door. Sunday dinner, I'd see them through the window sitting at the table, bowing their heads for a prayer. I'd even make up my own prayers. *Bless me Father and please let me wake up somewhere else with a different family.* Then I'd mumble some words in a language that I didn't know because they always seem to do that in prayers,' Hannah said.

'You're her only relative. Anyone found Mira yet?' Lex pulled out his car keys and looked at them.

'I don't know. I stopped answering my phone because they were asking too many questions. What did your mother do for work? Was she a drinker? Where is your father?'

'Simple, Hannah. Tell them the truth.'

'Which truth? The one where she goes around the whole day with chocolate syrup on her upper lip because she's decided that it's genius to have a lick of chocolate whenever she feels like it. Or maybe the one where she's a famous violinist who can't find her instrument and she walks up and down the street wailing about the Stradivarius she misplaced.'

'Didn't she tell you she wasn't long for this world last week?' Lex looked at his phone like an oracle.

'Something like that. Execution dream. Said someone wanted her to hang and she woke up coughing. Even told me she had bruises on her neck. Invisible bruises.'

Lex sighed.

'She rolled her socks into little balls and stacked them on top of her dresser in a triangle shape. Always a triangle. Remember how she'd cut spaghetti up with a knife until it looked like rice? Then she'd push it onto a tablespoon. Disgusting.'

Lex sighed again. When the phone rang, he grabbed it out of her hand before she could press the mute button.

'Hello. Yes. She's right here. A little distraught as you can imagine.'

Hannah snorted.

People die every day. Car accidents. Lightning strikes. Cancer or ALS. *Unnatural,* they said, as if death was supposed to be natural. All the letters and the basket of potpourri Sonya kept on her bedside table now existed without context. Books left unread, containers of forest berry yoghurt uneaten in the fridge, and her cat, now an orphan. Hannah detested cats.

Sonya's friend, Mira, was a psychic who told Sonya that she was chosen to be a deliverer of truth to a world gone haywire. Mira believed in mushrooms and root vegetables, the position of the stars and the direction of the wind. Sonya had a bear claw and the bone of an elk on her windowsill. She bowed to the north and always ate in a chair facing south. Hannah knew Sonya would not take her own life. She didn't have a terminal illness, at least not one that anyone knew about. She had just turned seventy-three.

Two weeks later, Mira showed up. The autopsy report had been entered into the record. A pathogen of unknown origin. More studies would be needed to determine its toxicity or if it could be contagious. Mira hugged Hannah. Her long violet and turquoise scarf wound around her neck so many times it made her head look as if it was floating atop her body.

'Your mother was one-of-a-kind, you know. Too bad her message didn't get out to more people. She worried about you, Hannah.'

Hannah moved her body outside the door. Mira smelled like patchouli and lavender. A huge rose quartz crystal hung from a velvet cord on her neck.

All of them would have to undergo tests.

'Don't know what kind of pathogen we're dealing with here,' the medical examiner said.

Sonya's computer looked like it was smashed with a hammer.

'Doesn't mean the hard drive isn't intact. Computer forensics is working on it,' the detective told them.

Hannah opened her umbrella even though it wasn't raining. There were cumulous clouds thick as loaves of bread above her.

Lex had gone back to work. He had important things to do that weren't about Hannah or Sonya. Nothing he did was about Hannah or Sonya and it never would be. She'd have the cat put down. Mangy orange thing. The cabin would go on the market as soon as they tested what they needed to test. They'd never find a thing; Hannah was sure of that. Sometimes people just die. Her uncle died assembling an Ikea dresser. Her baby brother drowned in a pond at the back of their house. Someone was supposed to be watching him.

Where is Drew, Hannah? Have you seen Drew?

It was a shallow pond but he was a small brother. Her grandmother died in her sleep, a good death, they said at the funeral. Hannah was seventeen and no one noticed how many cups of hot chocolate she drank at the luncheon after the funeral. It seemed as if her grandmother was only sleeping in the satin-lined box, her veiny hands clasping rosary beads. Everyone dies. What difference did it make how Sonya died? She'd be dead for the rest of Hannah's life and that was all that mattered.

Impossibly Small Spaces

My muscles had just started to unclench when the airplane bathroom door opened. I hid the vape pen behind my back.

'Sorry,' he took a few backward steps. I grabbed him by his loose-fitting sweatshirt and closed the door.

'We are experiencing turbulence and the captain has turned on the seatbelt sign. Please return to your seat.'

'Shhhh,' I said as we pressed together hovering over a toilet swishing blue-green liquid. Then I slid the lever to the lock position and blocked his hand with mine.

'Move,' he said.

He pushed but I was faster, covering the access with my body. My stomach gurgled and churned at the odour of urine and disinfectant.

'I hate flying.' I passed him the vape pen and he hesitated but took a hit. 'Give me a minute,' I said.

He went for the door again but I elbowed him, tamping down the animal in my chest.

'Fuck off. Just give me a minute,' I said. 'Do you want to get us both in trouble?' I pointed to the sign about smoke detectors and federal crimes as we lurched in a space the size of a refrigerator. The paper towel dispenser bumped my hip while he crouched by the toilet, head in his hands. He'd put the seat down and had one knee leaning on the plastic top.

'Please return to your seat immediately.'

He reached for the handle but I put my hand over his hand.

'There's nothing out there except pretzels and Coke,' I said, passing him the pen. He took another draw and smiled.

'People in Florida have pink plastic flamingos on their lawns and armadillos walk down the street. Poisonous snakes hide in the grass,' he said.

'Why are you going there?' I asked.

'Business.'

His mouth looked fleshy and he had the kind of eyes that seemed half-closed even though it was late morning. My age or older.

'What kind of business?'

'I work on an alligator farm.'

'Sure,' I said.

After I wrapped the pen in its pouch and slipped it in my pocket I unlocked the door. He rushed out. The flight attendant's mouth was a grim slash of red. I glared back at her and teetered down the narrow path to my window seat. The seat belt sign flickered off just as I heard the satisfying click of my buckle and slipped the ear buds into my ears. Ellen DeGeneres was prancing across the stage when he passed me a purple foil-wrapped Hershey kiss and a key. I put them on the tray table and closed my eyes for a second, envisioning myself walking down a street fringed with lacy magenta blossoms. When I opened them, he had conned the heavy-set woman next to me to switch seats. Since her ample midsection had been nudging me for the last two hours, I wasn't entirely unhappy.

'That took spunk,' he said. 'You're lucky I'm not the kind to turn you in.'

'You didn't seem to mind,' I said.

He laughed. 'Well, it was a first but what the hell. You from Florida?' He peered at me through those heavy-lidded eyes.

'Colorado. Going there to grow canna lilies and purple coneflowers. Maybe some hibiscus.'

'Liar,' he said, flashing a mouthful of expensively-straightened teeth.

'Good. Can I go back to watching *Ellen* now? She's about to have a dance contest.'

In my mother's cabin on Lake Goldstaff the closest town was Red Junction, population four hundred in a good year. And there weren't any good years. I had a water tank for showers but no septic so I used the outhouse all winter. Some days my bum would stick to the wooden seat and I imagined paramedics arriving by Jeep and using a blowtorch to pry me off, splinters and burns on my frostbitten cheeks. I awakened most mornings drenched with sweat and shaking. The reflections of aspens on the water, ice in the shape of footprints and my own hands spooked me. Then the whispers started. I would awaken certain that someone had entered the cabin. When I went through my mental contact list, I remembered my friend Rona in Boca Raton. I had supported her through a contentious divorce and sent cheery texts when she decided to start over in Florida. *Come and visit anytime.* I could sleep in her guest room for as long as it took me to figure things out. She had friends and a community.

The cabin was my only inheritance and I couldn't sell it. No one wanted to live in a town where you had to drive an hour to buy groceries and the temperature would freeze your nipples off from October to May. Anyone who could get out left before Thanksgiving. Mostly, I huddled by the woodstove reading or obsessing about how I came to be forty without health insurance, a pension or a relationship that lasted longer than six months. I recorded a message once a week just to hear my own voice and establish proof of my existence. Sometimes it took me minutes to catch my breath in the morning.

My mother had made a point of sharing the leather-bound journal of the cabin's history with me.

Built by a man who beat the shit out of his wife. When she finally had enough, she drugged him, rolled him into the lake while he was sleeping. Mountain justice for you.

I read all fifty-three pages, written in longhand by the wife. Did he awaken underwater; try to swim to the surface? For years, my mother fooled friends and neighbours with her homesteader advice. She carried a blanket and torch in her Jeep, nursed sourdough starter. Before Jack Daniels, there was wood splitting and sled-hauling and hot buttered rum for the neighbourhood on Christmas Eve. Before Jack Daniels she wore her grey hair in a twisted bun and owned a closetful of plaid Pendleton shirts. Before Jack Daniels she was an English teacher and sang in the choir at the Unitarian Church. After she lost the house in Durango a friend gave her the cabin.

He jostled my arm.

'What kind of soil do canna lilies need and what colour are they?'

'White. Sandy soil,' I said in my best gardener voice.

'Wrong. Pink or streaky orange. And they need a lot of water and pruning. Not a flower for the amateur,' he said, popping a chocolate into his mouth.

'Who says I'm an amateur? Mixing them up with calla lilies.'

'You know what I think? I don't think you're a gardener. You're going to Florida to get away from something – bad boyfriend or family.' He folded his arms across his chest as if congratulating himself.

'Brilliant deduction but wrong. What's your story? Are you from Florida?'

'No. Trying to win custody of my daughter from my slut of an ex,' he said, rolling his eyes.

'Why is everyone's ex a slut? Maybe she says the same thing about you,' I pushed the ear buds back in.

'No doubt. Anyway, she took Siobhan to Florida to live with her latest man. It won't last – the relationship, and Siobhan is alone too much. I worry about her.'

'What?' I pulled out one ear bud.

'Trying to scope it out, build a case.' He showed me a picture of a dark-haired teen in a sundress striking one of those faux sexy poses teenage girls think make them look older. Seriously gorgeous.

'You don't look like a detective,' I said.

This was the longest conversation I'd had in months.

He stuck out his hand, 'Neil McGovern, real estate.'

'Hildy Turner, not a gardener.'

'If you're not a gardener, what are you?'

'Still figuring that out. I vape and hike in reasonably warm weather.'

'For a living?'

I planned to work with traumatic brain injury patients before I went to Colorado to stop my mother from killing herself, a strategy that almost worked until she outwitted me by drinking herself to death and nearly killing me. I told him about the cabin and how I could see my breath on winter mornings. I omitted the part about Jack Daniels and the murder.

'We are beginning our descent into Palm Springs International Airport.'

I slipped my ear buds into my backpack and kicked it under the seat. The purple Hershey kiss and the key were still on my tray table, so I unwrapped the chocolate and ate it, handed him the key. He shook his head but took it.

If you're the kind of person who believes the universe will provide you with opportunity – one door closes and another door opens, there might be symbolism in a key. I'm the kind of person more likely to be killed in an avalanche.

Neil scribbled an address and phone number on a ripped off piece of the in-flight magazine.

'I know I should be mad at you but you seem kind of lost. This is in case you need something.'

'I need lots of things,' I said.

Neil put his hand on my shoulder for a second. My mother often draped her arm around me when she was drunk. *You smart shit. Why you wasting your time on me? Just let me die.* I'd guide her to the bathroom, pull a flannel nightshirt over her emaciated torso and she'd crawl out of bed later to fix another drink. Three months before she died, I awakened to her standing over my bed with a pillow. After that I locked my door at night and wedged a chair under the doorknob. A few times I could hear her breathing outside my door and once she tried the knob.

Solitude seemed perfect for personal growth but it was actually a kind of Miracle-Gro for depression. I had crying jags and went weeks without washing my hair. Last September a bear on the front stoop of the cabin wouldn't move when I needed to use the outhouse so I peed in a cup and poured it out the window, certain the bear would find a way in and maul me. The thought of my decomposing body discovered months later kept me up at night.

Once in the terminal I made a dash for the antiseptic multi-stall restroom. I hardly ever asked my smartphone for anything because I had one of those low data plans but I typed *Neil McGovern* and *Colorado* in Google and sure enough, there he was. There was even a rather flattering photo of him in a suit with his eyes mostly open. Real Estate. I typed in my own name because I was on a roll. Hildegarde S. Turner, MS, Neuropsychology, even a reference to my thesis on traumatic brain injury and links to articles written back when I thought publishing mattered. I dabbed water on my face, took deep breaths.

When I called Rona, her voice told me to leave a message.

Neil beat me to baggage claim and was picking up a rental car.

'Do you want a ride somewhere?'

I wanted a ride out of my life. Living in the margins had sharpened my features and made my hip bones jut out. The sale of my mother's stocks only supported me for about a year. I never sold the ruby ring my last girlfriend gave me back before she left for *a place with better vibes and reliable hot water*. I'm not sure why I got into his car. Maybe the simple answer was that I had nothing to lose.

'One bag?' an eyebrow raised as if I deliberately left the others in the airport.

Then he shrugged and hoisted it into the hatch, passed me the key.

On the drive to wherever, we passed palm trees, people wearing tropical prints and white shorts with sandals. I closed my hand around the key, pictured what it might open. Startlingly bright and humid, it seemed as if I'd ascended into a dimension where it was no longer an effort to breathe. Insects hummed and vivid blossoms bordered walkways.

He drew the vapour into his lungs like a scuba diver sucking in on the inhale before the slower exhale. I never understood my mother's craving for alcohol but I remembered the peace that came over her before the rages and migraines.

When Neil stopped to get a bottle of water, I tried Rona again, told her about my Google search and she said, 'good girl' like I was her retriever.

'Friends coming over later.' She mentioned her friend Kate. I pictured a trim body, straight blonde hair; conjured a massage therapist and gym membership. When I tried to disconnect, my finger pressed the wrong button and Rona laughed.

'Well, at least you figured out how to Google someone. I can show you apps for your phone later.'

Did I want the tiny screen of my phone cluttered with round-edged shapes offering weather, games, movies and hookups?

In the cabin I had a weak phone signal and no cable. I visited the library in the next town in good weather but mostly I dreamt of my own death. In the morning the sun skittered across the lake, and before fear paralysed me I'd bundle up to see the full moon. I slept with four pillows, pretending two were another person.

Then I saw the canna lilies. He was right. Raucously red-orange with a frill, they looked like irises dipped in paint. My winter eyes watered. I inhaled; took in chirps, hues, bicyclists and joggers, all going somewhere.

When he got into the car, he hunched over the water bottle like he was trying to light a cigarette.

'Time to move on,' I passed him back the key. 'Thanks for being a good sport about the vaping and all.'

'Hoping you'd stay.' He straightened up and looked straight at me.

Yanking open the car door, I crossed the street while he parked and wandered over to a bench. The door chimed and I inhaled freshly-baked croissants and cookies. I bought Rona six cookies that smelled like sun and bittersweet chocolate. When I held out a warm cookie to Neil still sitting on the bench looking at his phone, he didn't seem surprised, just handed me back the key.

'I thought we could go to a fish place I know for dinner. You do eat fish, don't you?' He stood up, brushed invisible lint off of his khaki slacks.

I nodded and bit into a cookie.

'You know, I could help you sell that cabin if you want. Wealthy people like that sort of thing. Unreachable.'

In good weather I had to stand on a chair to get my phone to work. Whorls of frost whited out the windows in winter and I'd huddle by the quarter of a pane where sunlight might break through. All of us leave our DNA everywhere we linger, a strand of hair or a flake of skin. Even the smallest of places can capture our secrets.

I linked my elbow through his.

'I'm a lesbian.'

'I like women too.' His eyes crinkled when he smiled.

The late afternoon sun was the colour of canna lilies. There were throngs of people walking, some coaxing dogs on pastel-coloured leashes. Teenagers poked at their phones, barely looking up. The air sizzled with energy and I felt like a dust mote caught up in the swirl. The swish of my sneakers synchronised with the tap of Neil's shoes. When he picked up the pace, I matched him step for step until we were skipping our way around skateboards, bicycles and dogs. I began laughing and he joined in, his shoulders quaking.

'Hildy. That's an old-fashioned kind of name,' he said.

'I'm an old-fashioned kind of lady.'

He slowed down in front of a yellow sign shaped like a crab. My stomach rumbled as if it finally recognised its function.

'I have a three-bedroom condo two blocks from the beach. Two of the bedrooms are ensuite.' He sounded like a realtor. 'Why don't you stay with me?'

I didn't answer.

We stepped into a grotto filled with the noise of competing conversations and the smell of fried seafood. At the burnished pine table we both reached for the breadsticks, bumping fingers. I bit into a garlicky breadstick while a guitarist strummed *Margueritaville*.

'Liddy. That's what I'm going to call you. Hildy sounds like someone's ancient aunt,' he said.

'Liddy?'

The whoosh and click of the ceiling fan reminded me of my snowshoes trekking across the frozen lake. Warmth pooled at the crown of my head and slowly seeped downward until there was a *plunk* that I thought for a moment Neil might have heard. It seemed as if I'd burst out of my skin.

Neil looked up. 'I made crappy choices with Siobhan.'

'Must be hard to raise a kid,' I said.

My mother loved stories and poems. We'd read aloud to each other on good days. Once she had loved my father enough to make a child.

'I should have fought for custody, stayed in better touch,' he said.

After my mother died, I talked to the lake because water has an enormous capacity for listening.

'Can we go to the beach after dinner?' I sipped my water and lemon.

Neil's expression softened. 'Sure. People gather there at dusk. Local folklore has it that this elderly couple would bring a cooler and wine to watch the sunset every night.

They'd toast and say *tomorrow*. One day, the wife said her husband's name instead of *tomorrow* and he died the next morning. That night she said her own name at the exact moment the sun disappeared. They found her in her bed, glass of wine still on the bedside table.'

'Is that supposed to be romantic? Sounds like a suicide pact,' I said.

'Maybe it's about the power of thought and having choices,' Neil said.

I have no idea who I am. Am I a daughter now that I no longer have a mother? In the woman's journal she wrote about her love for her husband. Even when she knew she'd kill him, she loved him. She just loved herself more. Before the cabin, I loved to fly. I would watch the roofs of houses turn to small squares, grassland sectioned into shades of green and gold.

Tomorrow I'd buy sandals and maybe shorts, a hat and sunglasses. A life with this much colour required a mute button. Definitely, I'd need sunglasses.

Scientia

When my right forefinger quit working during a math exam, Carlos explained.

'On holiday in Barcelona. Your digits are calculating the angles of the Basilica of the Sagrada Familia.' He tapped his fingers on an air calculator and pushed back a black thicket of hair that looked like a Rogaine advertisement.

'Manhattan is closer,' I said. Numbered streets in a grid had to be the pastime of a math genius.

Then my left ankle gave out during my second attempt at skiing. I guessed it would rather be lying on a beach in Key Largo. The young doctor who ace-bandaged me was humourless.

'Patch of ice or a mogul?'

'Bunny slope.'

'Don't ski,' he said, blinking rapidly as if the sight of my swollen ankle caused a foreign object in his eye.

For spring break Carlos had gone on a real vacation to Puerto Rico with his Uncle Miguel. He texted me a photo of turquoise water and a piece of some delicious fruit he was holding with working fingers. This morning I elbowed Angela Martin in chem lab and now she wouldn't share her notes from the class I missed.

'You have to be more careful. Think of our future employment, Carla.'

C & C – Carlos and Carla. Our virtual pharmacy.

We decided that my elbow was a bouncer in a biker bar, Angela's pink and spangled cardigan a direct affront. If she had shown up in leather maybe it would have behaved.

'Come home,' I said.

Memorising drug interactions did not constitute a life worth living. If he sent me any more azure and beige landscapes I'd start sending him photos of pill bottles. The drug store overflowed with students loading up on cough suppressants, analgesics and sunscreen for the anaemic sun. When he called during my lunch break I read him the names of the drugs I had packaged at work.

'Flonase, Gabapentin, Zoloft.'

'Elatra, Dolceavil, Mortrum,' he said.

'End your suffering forever with Mortum,' I said. 'Isn't that the drug used in Oregon for ...?'

'I think that's called Semper Somnus. The only one with a two-part name.'

Carlos texted me an emoji of a golden tropical drink with a paper umbrella.

'You made that up. The drug, I mean.'

'The point is, Carla, give your limbs what they need so they'll stop going on strike.'

'Paid time off?'

I stapled Arthur Patronsky's bag of Lipitor and Warfarin and rang them up along with Tums and a Snickers bar, ignored my co-worker's dirty look.

'My hand had better not decide it'd rather be in Scotland or on St John,' I said.

'Take your hand out for ice cream after work. Get a foot massage.'

I hung my white lab coat in the back and retrieved my backpack and bicycle helmet. The trees wouldn't shake into bloom for another two months but it was a teaser today – warm enough to summon the pucker of lemonade. At the walk-in clinic I told the doctor I was distracted by the sight of the first robin and didn't see the parked van at the edge of the pharmacy parking lot.

'Lucky you only hit the bumper,' she said, her white coat identical to the one I recently hung up. Pharmacist-in-training treated by a doctor-in-training. She smiled at me and I hoped her teeth were actually veneers glued over defective originals.

I wanted to receive a photo of my hand raising a pint at a pub in Galway. Instead, I was stuck scooping multi-coloured pills into an amber prescription bottle, capsules skittering across the counter.

Carlos texted me a picture of himself eating fried plantain and sofrito. He was wearing giant sunglasses. I told him I had to work tomorrow. My loans would eat up my income for the next twenty years. When I was an adequately-compensated pharmacist I would think about vacations that didn't include mouldy-looking sofrito.

'Your legs won't wait forever, Carla. You need recreation now.'

To Carlos, loans were pieces of paper that might burn in a fire, blow out the window of the car, if he had a car. Social Security numbers were meaningless computer printouts. He mulled over moving permanently to Puerto Rico since real estate prices fell after the hurricane. In two months he'd graduate, scope out defunct drug stores in warm climates. I'd join him a semester later or at least that was our plan.

'We can give away condoms. Lollipops after flu shots,' he said.

We decided we'd pitch some of our names to pharmaceutical companies. Firmitus for erectile dysfunction. Intrepida for anxiety.

My gauze-wrapped foot wouldn't fit into my toe clip. I would have to walk unless I could beg a ride. I tried motivational talks, promising mani-pedis and soaks in a tub I didn't have. My right hand had already begun to twitch and tingle so I made up drug names, Megaforte for low energy, Zentoma for high blood pressure, Robusto for iron deficiency, Actuenta for hallucinations.

The breeze evoked summer with its warm promises. Maybe Carlos had already located a pharmacy in Florida or Puerto Rico. I no longer cared. My hand tousled the curly hair of a man who definitely wasn't Carlos; a man looking at me with eyes like the sandy bottom of a riverbed. I wasn't sure how I came to be lying on navy-blue sheets with a window slightly open, Bob Marley wafting from a Bluetooth speaker. My mouth functioned without a hitch, legs tangled around his.

Although my sense of geography was spotty, I swear I caught sight of a palm tree and an orange-billed turquoise bird in my peripheral vision. The man sighed slightly, so I tested my appendages to make sure my fist wouldn't pop him in the eye or my leg knee him in the groin, but they were behaving. *This is what we've been waiting for,* they seemed to whisper as the curtain stirred and another absurd bird flapped red and yellow wings.

Blue Sock

Chelle thought I worked for legal services, the first of many untruths. She moved in without knowing anything, and that hasn't changed over the past two years. Love engenders safeguards. Janus said: *the less they know, the safer we are.* There is a reason why superhero stories use the cloak of anonymity. I shredded Janus' instructions and cut the envelopes into pieces when Chelle was showering or running errands.

The first time I picked up a padded envelope labelled *For Addressee Only* a white-haired woman pushed a grocery cart filled with bottles and cans and a teenager with a tattoo of Jesus on his forehead hauled a trash bag over his shoulder. Mounds of dirty snow piled up outside the post office and the American flag whipped back and forth in the wind. Why was I doing this? Justice? A fairer world?

Chelle and I had met while running on the path behind the high school. She called me *rhapsody in blue* because I was wearing shiny blue shorts and a blue shirt. When I returned to the same path we started running together.

Sweatpants and a down vest eventually replaced the shorts until the cold pushed me to the local community centre indoor track. When she showed up there, I knew the universe was tapping me on the shoulder, or in my case hitting me over the head with a 2 x 4.

'Seems like more than a coincidence,' I said, inviting her for lunch.

I rarely cook for myself. My work necessitates leaving at a moment's notice. We are the righteous ones, Janus told me. He has a lot of sayings like: *Doing the right thing does not always guarantee success* and *How you get there is not as important as getting there.*

At seven, my father left me in the car while he played craps. After a security guard found me, hungry and desperate to pee, I never again spent weekends with him. Four years ago my mother died and there wasn't much left after the funeral expenses, except whatever was in her safe deposit box. I kept the key in my bedside table drawer, tied inside a blue sock. *Be kind, Liam. Choose the higher ground,* my mother's note, scrawled on a ripped piece of yellow-lined paper.

Last summer we spent a week at Chelle's family cabin in Maine. When her father took us out on his boat she grabbed the slippery body of the fish she caught and tossed it back.

'Why'd you do that, Michelle? Would have made a nice meal. That was a bass. Your brother would have bagged that sucker. Rest in peace, Paul,' her father had said.

'Rest in peace, Paul,' Chelle repeated. Only sixteen when he veered off the road and hit a telephone pole.

She told me that she had never before considered that food on a plate could beg for breath and life, the hook in the mouth a cruel trick. I knew exactly how she felt.

When the sky opened up and we rushed to put away the fishing tackle, she said it reminded her of the rain during her brother's funeral. They stood freezing under umbrellas at the cemetery. After that her mother lost interest in her job and even family gatherings. No one was surprised when she had a massive stroke at fifty-seven. But her father went on fishing in Maine in the summer and now he was dating a woman he had met online.

Chelle lost her job at the museum three months ago. I told her it was probably for the best. Favouring shirtwaist dresses in floral patterns, paired with tights and lace-up pastel-coloured boots she seemed to have materialised from another time period. She was the kind of woman Degas or Modigliani might have painted, porcelain skin and hair like a blonde cloud framing her face. I encouraged her to apply for a job at the local re-enactment village where she could dress in period clothing, channel a simpler time.

What did I want? Opportunity? Less violence? More love?

After the last attack, Janus stepped up our game. This week's envelope held a map and plane ticket, just in case.

'The company is reassigning me. I'll have to travel more,' I said.

Chelle looked up from putting the casserole in the oven. She adjusted the scarf she tied on her head to keep her wild blonde hair out of her eyes while she was cooking.

'How much more?'

'Hard to say,' which struck me as one of those stupid answers that communicate nothing.

'What are you working on?'

Fortunately, she was one of the least curious people I know. She did not believe in prying, though she deserved more than my cursory explanations. Staying alert and in the present offered protection for both of us. The less she knew, the better.

'This and that. Saving the world,' I said, putting broccoli in the steamer.

Chelle laughed. 'I believe it. You have a way of convincing people. Me, for example. I mean, I hardly knew you and here we are living together.'

I massaged her shoulders. She always has this trigger point on the right side under her shoulder blade.

'Ouch!'

'That one is a doozy,' I said, working it with my fingers.

'Mmmm.' It softened under my touch and she turned to kiss me.

'Any luck with the re-enactment village job?'

'Interview next week,' she said.

We both knew that this kind of job would go nowhere. Chelle had dreams of being a curator in a museum. Dreams matter.

'You know I'll support you until you find work. If it is money you're worried about, we're fine,' I said.

My phone vibrated several times during dinner. Finally I pretended I had to go to the toilet and checked: Janus. An attack in a different city. When I returned to the kitchen I slurped water directly from the tap, wetting the front of my shirt.

'Let's go out for a drink,' I said.

At the hewn maple table at our favourite pub I took baby steps toward sharing.

'About six years ago a man asked me if I cared more about money or the future of the planet. You probably know my answer. Most of what I do won't change things drastically but something happened today. For every person or group working to save a species, cure a disease or clean up the environment, there are two to three groups trying to take them down,' I said.

She put her hand on mine for a second, then twisted her hair with her thumb and forefinger and sipped the dark ale. She would not ask me any questions. Instead we talked about Maine, fishing and her collection of beach glass.

Chelle spent many hours as a child and adult walking along the beach, looking for periwinkles, oyster shells and beach glass. On our kitchen windowsill a small jar of beach glass caught the sun in the morning. She collected blue, green or red glass and told me how she tested the sharpness against her palm. Perfect beach glass had smooth edges battered by the tide. Once, a triangle-shaped cobalt blue fragment drew blood, but she said she kept it anyway, buried amid the benign remnants.

We linked fingers on the table.

'I'll empty the safe deposit box on Monday,' I said.

Chelle looked at me with her old soul eyes and nodded.

'Can we use the cabin in Maine?'

'I guess. The woodstove keeps it warm enough and Dad only uses it in the summer.'

When we got home we packed only what would fit in the car.

'I don't want to know what you do. I'm proud of you no matter what,' she said.

She nestled in my arms and we stood there holding each other. The life we had made: books, clothes, a jar of beach glass and a wool blanket fit into three boxes.

We arrived at the bank as soon as it opened and a woman with painted-on eyebrows said, 'We were going to drill the box at the end of the month. You have to pay the bill, sir.'

She narrowed her eyes and slowed her speech as if speaking to a child.

Chelle waited in a grey upholstered chair while rain dripped down the windows.

The flesh-coloured plastic top made the box look small but it was long and deep. I thought of magicians pulling scarves and rabbits out of hats as I snapped it open and found cardboard jewellery boxes, cotton pouches, a manila envelope and a moleskin journal. One pouch contained a hand-carved pipe and what we used to call a buttercup, that almost translucent orangey-gold shell all over Maine beaches. A box held a diamond ring I only remember seeing once or twice on my mother's hand. I had assumed my father pawned it or they sold it to pay expenses. Assorted earrings and costume jewellery were in the other boxes. I didn't open the envelope or the journal. Instead I dumped everything into a small daypack.

When we got to the car I pulled out the diamond ring with its old-fashioned setting.

'Stingiest bastard you'd ever meet, my father. I got socks and briefs for Christmas. Mother must have stashed this away. Smart woman, my mother, to keep this away from him. It would have gone to the casino.' I passed the ring to Chelle.

I opened the envelope and another moleskin notebook tumbled out. I dabbed away tears and blew my nose on the sock I left on the front seat. Chelle put her hand on my shoulder, stroked my back. Then my phone pinged and pinged again.

Rain continued to blur the car windows as we sat there in the parking lot before I started the car, cranked up the defroster.

A stranger peered in the passenger window, pressing his face against the glass, fish-like eyes and a black umbrella. Then he rapped on the window with a pinky ring. I slammed the car into reverse and floored it, the umbrella flying out of the man's hand, handle facing up like a crooked finger.

'What? Who is he, Liam?' Chelle shivered next to me.

'Don't want to find out.'

By the time we hit the interstate, fog bore down, a bear paw swatting the windshield. I had placed the diamond ring on her finger.

'Marry me,' I said, turning away from the road for a second. 'I promise I'll tell you more after we get to Maine.'

My fingers gripped the steering wheel so hard my knuckles turned blue-white.

Windshield wipers clapped back and forth, barely keeping up with the misty rain.

'Ok. Yes.' Chelle leaned in, her shoulder pressing against mine.

I felt the knot in my back loosen. She could garden, make soup in the wintertime and apply for a real museum job. I looked at her looking at the ring and smiled.

The murkiness gave way to true darkness, rain intermittent but persistent enough that our conversation was punctuated by the swish and tap of the windshield wipers. Chelle had her hand on my thigh. Even a short time in the cabin with its pine furniture and exposed beams would be welcome, and Chelle would be safer there. She passed me a bottle of water. I fiddled with the radio but static dominated.

In the rearview window I saw headlights behind us growing closer, two yellow eyes staring us down.

'We're being followed,' I said in a barely-audible voice. Janus told me to separate myself from the work. How many perfect days ruined – 9/11, the Boston Marathon, my engagement? *Casablanca*. In the grand scheme, if there is one, our own problems don't amount to much.

I accelerated and the car behind me matched my speed.

'Call your father,' I told her.

She protested but I did not back down.

'I can't drag you into this. There's a town in a mile or so.'

She pressed her boot down on the floorboard as if she could step up the pace. We watched the yellow headlights like the eyes of a sea monster bouncing off the rearview mirror. I could almost read the licence plate. Michigan. He came a long way to find me. I switched lanes but a few seconds later the eyes tracked me again.

'I can't go any faster,' I said, breathing through my fear the way I'd been trained.

Then I heard the siren. Great. How the hell am I going to explain this? I saw flashing blue lights but the yellow headlights were gone.

'Pulled over.' Chelle said. 'You lost him.'

I know it made her feel safer but these people carry excuses in their wallets. At most it would buy us a few minutes. The next exit had a food and lodging sign and I left Chelle at a Motel Six. Her father would arrive in three hours.

'You sure we need to do this?' Her eyes, bloodshot from crying, words all slurred together.

'Yes,' I said, though uncertainty wound around me like a cord. I told her to sign in under another name and lock the door.

'Call me when your father gets here,' I said, 'Have him call you when he is at the door. Promise me you won't open the door for anyone else.'

He's waiting for me. Maybe not the same *him* but another of his ilk. What did I expect? We pretend that one way is right but even Janus knows that is an illusion. We are the same. Right now I want more than anything to take Chelle in my arms. Instead I head back to the highway, my headlights gleaming on the wet road, the fog bearing down.

The Price

My brother Gene believes that numbers don't lie and the greater than fifty percent divorce rate in the United States means that more than half of us have chosen the wrong mate, even if we won't know it for years, a factoid he offered while I moved the crusts of my BLT around the crockery plate.

'Why don't you eat crusts? Even my kids eat crusts,' he said at the restaurant where we met to discuss Mother.

'I don't like them. Besides I'm full.'

Gene's plate was empty. Not a crumb. He doesn't like waste, hated there to be even a sip of coffee left. I had at least a quarter of a cup growing cold in the floral mug.

Lilac-scented breezes wafted through the window with its broken screen and chips of what was probably lead-based paint on the sill. The scent brought me back to Nantucket, that lush island off Cape Cod where I moved like a vapour around the rich at the Tides Resort one summer. My brother and I have rules about what we'll share, which is why I never told him what I did. Outside men drove little carts around the golf course while inside

Filipino women with creases around their eyes wheeled freshly-laundered towels, sheets and miniature soaps up and down the corridors. A college student, I was only slightly elevated in the order of hired help, a distant relation. The women vacationing there wore starched tennis skirts with bright blouses that showcased tanned, muscular arms. Thick woven gold adorned necks and slender wrists and diamonds the size of my pinky nail glinted in the sunlight.

At twenty I was skinny with a red-tipped braid dangling down my back and a wardrobe that consisted of two shirts with the crest of the Tides Resort emblazoned over the pocket, pressed black pants, one t-shirt, jeans and a green bikini for my day off when I'd beg José the prep cook for a ride to Madaket to swim or catch the sunset. Sociology major, I fancied myself conducting research on the rich, the ones who got lucky on the stock market, inherited a trust fund or made a business decision that paid off. They would order me about while looking over my head as if scanning for someone more worthy.

'Phoebe. Decaf with one equal. That's a decaf, Phoebe. Equal.'

I heard you the first time, bitch, I would think as I trotted into action, traversing the slate walkway by the pebbled garden with its profusion of roses, chrysanthemums and other blossoms I couldn't name. More than once I was tempted to use the caffeinated pot, see if the bitch would actually rise from her chair. When I brought the coffee back to Mrs Julia Rathbun reclined on a chaise lounge with the latest Danielle Steele novel, she nodded and pointed to the table.

Our mother was too far into dementia nowadays to remember the chain of events that unfolded, how I wasn't invited back the next summer, even though I was not one of the six called in for questioning. They wanted to do a clean sweep, ensure that the riff-raff who committed the deed wouldn't sully their island again. Plenty of us to go around.

'Phoebe, we've got to figure this out.' Gene pulled me back. He pushed the paint chips into a pile and I was thinking that lead poisoning lowered your IQ. Still I couldn't tell a grown man not to play with lead-based paint any more than he could force me to eat my crusts.

'Mother is running out of money.'

Though Gene is an estate lawyer, he looked more like a short-order cook, greasy-haired and cheaply dressed in a striped shirt and chinos. He even picked his teeth and wiped it on the napkin. He had been handling Mother's money for the last two years, a relief for me since I barely managed to do my own taxes.

'What do you want me to do? You're the rich one,' I said.

'Me? I've got Liz and the kids to think about. All you've got is a dog.'

'God, Gene. I'm a teacher. You know what I get paid?'

For the record, Ingrid wasn't just a dog. She represented the longest relationship I've ever had. She was content to watch *Adam's Rib* with me for the tenth time, didn't mind if I cried and she never asked me to stop hanging bras over the shower rod.

At the time I felt justified in taking the five thousand. Pocket change to these people. They dropped hundreds in the gift shops on the island, stocking up on Nantucket bags, those basket pocketbooks with scrimshaw on the top. Mrs Julia Rathbun was in her thirties, about my age now. Dark hair swept back in a stylish ponytail. Who has that kind of cash just lying around? I saw the open box through the French doors while she was tanning herself, oblivious to skin cancer or wrinkles.

'Ice water, Phoebe. That's ice water. Extra ice.'

Do I look deaf? I'd think. So easy to slip in the door from the other side, come back minutes later with her tall glass of water. She even told me about the theft, suspecting the Salvadoran gardener or the Filipino chambermaid, not me, a nice white college girl. We don't steal. I'm sure her insurance covered the whole thing but it ate away at me. I'd awaken at night with her unnaturally green eyes staring.

I kept the money in a locked metal box for a year. Then I bought a used Honda Civic, crashed it six months later. The insurance money came to five thousand.

The day we decided to move Mother to Willoughby's Senior Apartments the weather turned and it was cold and windy. I would have stayed in denial a little longer but Gene pressed me.

'She left the stove on last week. She lost the diamond bracelet Pat gave her and stopped locking the door because she can't figure out how keys work, when she can find them.'

I dabbed my eyes on a stupid checkered napkin. The end of an era. Once I envied Mother. She had a social ease and men loved her. I figured she'd just find another after Pat had a heart attack putting up insulation in the attic. Each husband was progressively richer. Mother met Pat at a church fundraiser. They'd send me postcards from St Martin and Bermuda. I'd meet them at a stylish bistro and unwrap a little box with overpriced earrings from some island. I don't know when it became apparent that Mother wasn't finding anyone else. I guess Gene figured it out before I did.

We moved her in December, rented a U-Haul and Gene distracted her by taking her to see *Hidden Figures*. When I cleared out the house, I found the diamond bracelet in a silk pouch under the bed. Later I took it to a jeweller to be appraised and it turned out to be cubic zirconia. Guess the rich ones can fool you.

I almost shared the Nantucket story with Mother after my divorce but I guess I was holding out for a time when I wasn't already a loser in her eyes. Her mascaraed lashes fluttered when I told her maybe it was better to be single.

Hard to imagine her running out of money. Pat owned a chain of appliance stores, Rooney's Electronics with the 'Looney Deal of the Month'. He sold me a washer and dryer *for cost,* had it delivered. Sure, he could have afforded to give it to me but you don't get stinking rich from giving stuff away.

'We've got two options, Phoebe. Move her to state-subsidised assisted living which you know she'll hate or pay to keep her at Willoughby's with a caregiver.' My big brother was the king of options. As a kid he'd make lists of choices.

'If we go to the beach we can use our raft, if we camp we can have a campfire and toast marshmallows.' Pros and cons. Dos and Don'ts. I can just see him with Liz. 'If we go to bed by nine we can make love tonight. If we go to bed at ten we will have to wait until Saturday.' I'm hopeless at decision-making. That's why he makes so much more money than I do.

'She loves Willoughby's.'

'Caregivers are twenty dollars an hour.' Gene was chewing on his fingernails, badly in need of cutting.

'Can we get by on four hours a day?' I said.

'It only buys us a little time. She is down to $10,000.'

'Doesn't she get Dad or Jed or Pat's survivor's benefits?'

'Geez, Phoebe. You think that is much of anything?' Still chewing on those bloody fingernails. She had three husbands. You think she'd get a bonus for that.

Pat left most of his sizeable estate to his kids from his first marriage. Mother thought there was some mistake. She loved him. Gene checked it over and over. Ironclad. Guess you never really know another person. Even after he told her there was nothing she could do, Mother insisted Pat must not have been in his right mind. She *forgave* him.

'She's eighty-nine,' I said.

'Actuarial tables say that if you live to be eighty-nine, your chances of living to ninety-five are better than sixty percent.'

How does he know this stuff? He was the nerd in the back of the class, calculating the statistical probability of a snow day to determine if he'd have to take his Advanced Placement Calculus exam the next day.

It's not like I wanted Mother to die. I liked her world better than mine. She asked about my job and told me I worry too much about my students, which is true. I used to dread visiting her, especially after she blamed the divorce on me and told me that I disappointed her.

'A woman has to keep her man interested. Why don't you do something different with your hair?'

I failed to see the relationship between my hair and my ex's need for variety but I tried highlights and a haircut. Ingrid barked at me and the man I found online smelled like a hog farm. I spent Saturday nights binge watching *The West Wing*.

'Phoebe. I wish you would take this seriously. I figure if we each kick in $300 a month we can keep her at Willoughby's a little longer.' Gene took off his glasses and cleaned them by dipping his napkin in his water glass.

'Not equitable. You make way more than I do. How about you kick in $500 and I kick in $100? I have a mortgage, too.'

'Fine.'

It was disappointing to have him cave so easily. I wanted to produce pay stubs and tell him about Ingrid's hip surgery. Then I got it. He *knew* I would only end up paying $100 or maybe even $50. It was a ploy, that stolen money coming back to haunt me. It would take four years to spend down my curse, the universe's way of righting itself. Gene's actuarial table predicted at least four more years.

I could have asked for an accounting of where my hundred dollars went each month, but I didn't. Mrs Julia Rathbun trusted me not to steal her five thousand dollars and I trusted Gene because I assumed he was smarter and richer. I'm sure my brother sleeps well. *If Phoebe kicks in a little she'll feel included.* Some things we never talk about, like the way he took my ex's side after the divorce or the three times it took him to pass the bar exam.

Four years and three months later, standing on a chair in my classroom stapling prints for our Greek mythology unit, I got the call. They found Mother on the floor of the craft room clutching her chest, perfectly-applied eyeliner and lipstick and not a hair out of place. Ten thousand still in the bank and a will that stated that we were to split everything. Fifty-fifty.

Scorpion

Not even nine o'clock and everything spinning like that doomed farmhouse in *The Wizard of Oz*. Metal against metal and then an explosion after the black Lexus plowed into the side of her car, glass strewn across the seat like confetti. Searing pain and a bang as the airbag inflated. She landed on her back in a clearing where Casey had once crouched in her favourite pink shorts to pick up a snakeskin, sneakers crunching over branches.

Last summer they found a snake with reddish brown markings sunning itself on a rock by the path behind the house. When she looked it up on her phone it looked most like an Eastern Milk Snake, gorgeous but harmless.

'Look. The old skin.'

Slightly translucent and intact, it was onionskin thin, camouflaged on dried leaves. Her ex, Doug, never would have spotted it, or if he did he would have kicked it aside. Thankfully the snake slithered into the underbrush before Casey had a chance to touch it or ask to keep it as a pet.

'Maybe we'll find a rattlesnake,' Casey had said.

'Nothing poisonous.'

Ava understood Casey's desire to see the object of so much fear up close. She had a fascination for spiders like the brown recluse and black widow. She knew scorpions like to hide in shoes and the unsuspecting victim just slips them on, blindly going through the routine, except on this day, the foot would sting and swell up, while the victim's blood pressure drops. Scorpion stings kill more people than snakebites.

When Ava returned her to Doug, a hollow space inside her chest opened up. The house without her sneakers running up and down the hallway and her trill of laughter seemed lifeless. Ava walked by her room, touched her collection of plastic reptiles and straightened her two pillows, one with a shark pillowcase and the other with lizards. Better schools in Doug's district so she stayed there during the week, came to Ava every weekend and Ava had to fight for that. Since most of Casey's friends lived near Doug she sometimes asked to stay with him on the weekend. They had resolved not to put her in the middle or hamper her life with their issues but last night they had argued.

'Casey said you brought work home. Is that how you spend your weekends with her? We could have taken her to Judith's parents' house on the lake.'

'I don't have to justify how we spend our time. That's my business.'

Ava had goals, like buying a summer cottage in Wellfleet. Worth the sacrifice to finally have something to show for her hard work.

'One, two, three, lift. Careful with the leg.'

Someone put what looked like bubble wrap around her leg, hoisted her in the back of an ambulance. She could hear the siren but it sounded like she was underwater, kind of a shriek and then a gurgle. Her left leg throbbed. No, throb wasn't the right word for it, more like a burn.

She screamed and moaned before everything went black again.

When she came to, a dark man with wide black-brown eyes that looked like they were rimmed with eyeliner was looking at her, dreamy exotic eyes. If this was death, so far, it wasn't bad except for the searing pain.

'She's coming to. We'll give you something.' He placed a hand on her arm, a sudden heat where his fingers touched her skin.

'Can you hear me? I'm Dr Malik. You've hurt your leg and there's a deep laceration on your left arm. Don't move.'

An electric pain twisted and stabbed her leg, her arm singing a sharp achy song. Ava wasn't about to test her fortitude by moving. Her throat felt thick and constricted, heartbeat like the little tree frog she held in the palm of her hand last summer.

'Can I keep him, mommy?' Casey had asked.

'No. It's not fair to take him out of his habitat. You can hold him for a minute but then you need to let him go.'

Casey's face had crumpled and then turned dark.

'Do you think he has babies? Does he live with his family? Does he like us?'

All questions she couldn't answer so she led Casey back to the house and tried to interest her in a snack of cookies and milk.

'The pain medication should kick in soon. Do you know where you are?'

Ava nodded, though she wasn't sure. A hospital?

'We're going to move you in a little while. Is there someone you want us to call?'

Her only sibling, Esther, lived far away in Poughkeepsie. Her father was in assisted living. Casey.

Casey was with Doug. Doug. For a moment Ava assumed that Dr Malik could hear her thinking.

'Is there someone you want us to call?' He repeated himself in that baritone voice with the slight accent.

Phone. Where was her phone?

He read her mind.

'Your phone and other things are in a bag at the end of the gurney. We can give them to your friend or relative. You're going to be here a while.'

Pam had been telling her she needed a vacation.

Dr Malik returned to tell her that he hadn't been able to reach anyone except Pam.

Then Doug was at Ava's bedside; tie askew, his face earnestly bending to hers.

Dr Malik turned to her.

'Do you know him?'

'Ava. I'm so sorry.'

Doug looked at Dr Malik.

'Can I speak to the doctor? Doug Tremblay, Ava's ex-husband.'

'Dr Ahmed Malik,' he stuck out his hand but Doug looked at Ava.

'I'll keep Casey. Don't worry.'

She could see where this was going. He wanted Casey full-time.

'Will she be ok?' Doug asked, absolute model of ex-husbandly concern.

'I can't answer that. We'll know more after surgery.' Dr Malik's voice was silken, golden cows with bells around their necks shuffling through a dusty courtyard.

'Are you a surgeon?' Doug asked.

'Yes.' Dr Malik turned to the nurse who was setting up an intravenous.

The pain waltzed with the medication, wrapped around her, a knife-wielding shadow; trail of sparks that stuck out their red tongues at the edge of her sight. A woman with a print uniform that looked like it had multi-colored hotdogs dancing on it, adjusted the IV bag on a pole. For a moment, Ava thought the pole was a scarecrow and she scanned it for the face. It's the face that scares away the crows. Another woman with hundreds of tiny braids and the same hotdog print uniform glided alongside her gurney.

'They're ready for her in O.R., Dr Malik.' It sounded like *Oroboros, Dr Magic.* Ava flinched and swatted away what looked like an iridescent fly. Doug touched her hand again.

Before Pam dashed to her side, Ava could hear her sensible heels clicking from the end of the hallway.

'Oh God, Ava. What happened?' Pam nodded curtly to Doug.

'I guess I'll take off now. You take care of yourself, Ava.' Doug kissed her on the forehead with lips she once French-kissed through the entire first Batman movie.

Her mouth felt swollen, so she blinked and gave a small head movement, the best she could muster.

A nurse interrupted them.

'The waiting room is that way.' Tiny braids and orange sneakers. Orange like some of the little hotdog shapes.

Lights flickered as the gurney glided through an open door.

Ava thought the light looked like a snakeskin curled onto itself. As she fell under, she saw a younger version of her mother warning her. *Don't marry him, Ava.* Her sister Esther picked up a snakeskin to show to a drug-free doppelganger of her nephew chewing gum and balancing on one sneakered foot and then another. Doug came out from behind a fir tree with that smile, the one that disarmed her. His arms opened wide for a hug but he had on some kind of prickly shirt that scratched her bare arms bloody. He said he still loved her as much as he did on their honeymoon in Positano.

'We're lucky, Ava. Most people never find the right person.'

Ava had pushed for the pregnancy because she was thirty-two and their kind of luck called for a child.

'Ms Tremblay. Are you propositioning me?'

'Absolutely, Mr Tremblay.'

Then everything started to irritate him – her demitasse collection, Esther's late night phone calls, the way she picked the tomatoes off her salad and drenched it in ranch dressing. His eyes would cloud over and he'd run his hand through his hair as if her presence somehow caused him to be dishevelled. She could have adapted to that but his carelessness with Casey scared her. He'd toss her in the air, let her play in the front yard while he read a book.

'She's a toddler, Doug. She needs supervision every minute,' Ava told him.

'Just because your parents hovered over you doesn't mean we have to do that with Casey. I don't want her growing up neurotic,' he said.

When he accused her of having an affair with an old college friend, they agreed to divorce. Casey was three. One moment they were planning trips they wanted to take, a second child, and the next she was a single businesswoman, socking away money for a solo retirement.

Ava's eyes opened to white walls and little metal bars on the bed. There was a pink plastic tray with a pitcher on it and a flat-screen TV hanging from the ceiling, a rectangle of blackness. Her leg was in some kind of traction device and her left arm wrapped in a gauzy bandage, right arm anchored to an IV where something dripped into her vein. A rectangle of sunlight on the cotton blanket; one tree visible from the window, green leaves edged in brown. The pain had boxing gloves and boots, swatting and stomping. She screamed and a young man ran in, grabbed a clipboard.

'Ava Stinson? Are you having pain? You've only been out of surgery a few hours. It's normal. Dr Malik will be in soon to talk to you.'

When she closed her eyes, she could see Casey again.

'Can we get a kitten? Daddy and Judith said I could get a kitten. I want to name him Sandy.'

She awakened to Dr Malik smiling at her.

'You're a lucky woman. The laceration just missed a major artery. It's a bad break in your leg and it will be months before you can put any weight on it. The good news is that there isn't any permanent damage. The bad news is that you'll have a large scar. The police have been by and will come back to ask you a few questions about the accident. They haven't found the driver yet. Oh and Doug called.'

Ava couldn't stop the hot tears once they started.

'I know it's a lot to handle. Every challenging experience has something to teach us, yes? You're alive, Ava. Life will not be the same but different is not always bad.'

She didn't believe him.

'When can I go home?'

'You'll be here at least two weeks. Then you'll go to rehab. By mid-winter you should be walking on crutches and by summer, you can be free of all of it, if everything goes according to plan. But the first rule is: nothing ever goes according to plan.'

When Pam accompanied her to Billingsford Rehabilitation, the leaves were riotous on the trees, spread like gaudy scarves on the cooling ground. Push and pull. Every action had a reaction. There were balls and pulleys, special chairs and treadmills. Callouses developed on her hands from gripping the handrails but she could take a few steps with support now. Dr Malik visited a couple of times.

'They say you'll be ready for crutches in another week or two.' He touched her hand lightly.

The rehabilitation folks bought her a cupcake every time she reached a new goal – wheelchair to walker, walker to crutches. In late November, it was time to go home with daily visiting nurse support. Handles had been installed on the tub. A new normal. A day with less pain was a good day. Work was making coffee, hobbling to the table with the French press and getting the mail from the mailbox at the end of the driveway.

The first request for full custody came on a Tuesday. *That bastard.* Ava asked for an extension because she couldn't yet drive. The police were still looking for the driver of the Lexus. The car and its driver seemed to have vanished like that Malaysian airliner.

Ava requested a joint custody that included having Casey on Tuesday and Thursday nights. When she told Doug, he cleared his throat and then he started in.

'Casey has friends here. Why don't we ask her what *she* wants? She has her kitten to take care of. Besides, you need more time to recover.'

'I'm doing fine.'

Then she received a summons. He was going to have doctors testify about her physical inability to handle an active eight-year-old.

The jagged scar that went from the front of her thigh to the back of her knee turned an angry purple and then a calm white. Dr Malik told her how he used all of his skill as a surgeon to minimise the damage. After a while Ava got used to it, the way a tattoo becomes a part of the skin's legend. She stood in front of her full-length mirror naked and it seemed as if an intricately-patterned snake had wound its way around her right leg, swallowing his own tail.

A book on spiders was due to arrive in the post in time for Casey's visit tomorrow. Even though the temperature had dropped overnight, Ava left her coat over the bannister and walked to the mailbox. She didn't see the glaze of ice until her legs splayed out and shock waves shot through her back and thighs. Rolling onto her side, she propped herself up on one elbow, spasms of pain rippling. The empty bucket lay on its side by the garage door, garden hose unravelled like a snake.

CONSORTS

Angel's mother is a special kind of superstitious. Everyone knows that Angela is the feminine form of Angel but she's named Angel after a stillborn brother. This is where it gets complicated. He was christened Bryant but because he's presumably an angel and her mother became pregnant again immediately, she got stuck with being the reincarnation of her dead brother. See what happens when religion sucks all the logic from your brain? *#notabeliever*

We're cross-legged on Angel's leopard print bedspread, her last four phones spread out in front of us. She's got the phone thing down. Tells her mother that her latest stopped working and she gets a new one. I'm at least three models behind her. I pick up her iPhone 6.

'Can't you sell these on eBay?'

Angel gives me that look she reserves just for me – kind of *do you even live in 2018?* combined with *do I look like I need the money? #friendswithmoney*

'Lulu, your father needs you to pick up milk on the way home.' Angel's mother pokes her blonde head in the bedroom door. Her hair looks like a bathing cap, sleek and the colour of dandelions. I wonder if a hairdresser convinced her this was a good look. I nod, hoping she'll go away. Angel gives me a half-smile because we both think her mother is more than a little off, kneeling before all those tables she has set up with pictures of the Blessed Virgin and Jesus. It ruins the flow of the house, kind of an anti feng shui.

I don't think my father cares about milk. He's just checking to see if I'm really at Angel's house. After three letters from school informing him of my unexcused absences, he makes feeble attempts to monitor where I am. He's stealthy, my Dad, pretending to need help moving furniture or fixing the screen on the porch so I'll stick around. Once, he saw me put a jackknife in my backpack before walking to the bus. *#secretplan*

'I don't need you getting suspended from school, Lulu.'

In the old days, he'd ask me what my mother would think but he doesn't go there anymore. Neither of us believes she's perched on a fluffy cloud with a harp, watching over us. *#deathisntfair*

I thought for sure Angel would ask Lucien to the sophomore dance but she brought Sylvie instead, so I took my Dad. He even rented a tux. We like to be outside what's trending. *#killingit*

That event was the finale of two years of practice, from the Halloween I snooped to find her costume (she was a checkerboard, I came as a pair of dice) to our flash dance duo of 'Singing in the Rain' in the lunchroom, both of us holding up paper drink umbrellas while the lunch monitors ran around trying to regain control. I didn't see her pretend conversion to Judaism coming and she never guessed my two-week vegan phase was fake. *#animalcruelty*

That jack-knife came in handy when I picked her locker to leave a croissant, linen napkin and a plastic wine glass of cranberry juice. *#breakfastofscholars* If one of us anticipates something about the other, we change it up. *#consortsinwhimsy*

'Privacy. Remember when that was a thing?' Angel unbuttons her top button. Her socks are the colour of blood except for the splatters of black. Kindergarten finger-paint socks. No, I don't remember. My phone knows everything I'm doing and it doesn't even have facial recognition or a functioning microphone. *#notalone*

When Dad gets married again, I'll spend more time with Angel. Her parents don't notice and their house has more rooms than anyone needs plus television with hundreds of channels.

'Do you think about dying?' Angel's eyes are chocolate lab brown.

'Course. You?' I found my mother's purple *Fuck Cancer* hat the other day, hung it over the side of my mirror. Toward the end she traded righteous rage for sadness and that was the worst. It made me start smoking even though I knew she could smell it. She always said I had a snake inside of me and I'd need to charm it before it choked me. I promised to get good grades, help Dad organise the garage and pull up the weeds and little brown mushrooms in our yard. I've accomplished none of those things, though I did find her journal in a box next to antifreeze and motor oil. Sometimes I think I'll publish it for her. Other times it's too hard to read about her fear of losing her *essence* and her hair turning to *wisps of dried grass. #cancersucks*

'My fam is getting ready for the dead bro ceremony.' Angel twists her hair and picks at her already beat-up cuticles.

A special Mass for Bryant was held every year at St Justin's Church. We went because it was a way to show respect, though Angel and I talked more about the refreshments her parents ordered from Sweet Things Bakery. Even though it had been years, they hauled in a bulletin board of family photos. Because he was a stillborn, there weren't any pictures of him but there was seriously one of his room.

'We need to shake something. YOLO, Lulu.' She messes up her brown-black curls. My hair lays flat except when I borrow gel and we spike or muss it.

'Yeah. Carpé Diem.'

Truth is, I'm not down with interrupting someone's religious moment even if I think it's some made up shit. Her mother just about had a breakdown and if the Blessed Virgin and Jesus are helping her to keep it together, fine.

'But I like your mother.' Not really. Maybe she was smart before Bryant died. Our mothers never would have been friends. Even the day before she died my mother turned away a visit from the pastor.

'I'd prefer the Dalai Lama. I don't need to pray. I need to breathe and look at the sky.'

Dad still refers to the Dalai Lama as Mom's conversion. When I'm in one of my moods and don't want to talk, he calls it a Zen moment.

The wedding is going to be in Vermont at some inn. I get it that Dad should have sex and someone to keep him company but not Freesia. At first he told me that she was the 'best of the worst'. Then she became 'better than most' and they got engaged.

'Your mother's been gone five years,' he said as if that was the magic time to find a new wife. Maybe this one comes with a better warranty. Freesia is thirty-eight and my Dad is forty-six. She's divorced and doesn't have kids so there could be a half-sibling in my future. It reads like a bad romance novel.

'Remember when I brought Sylvie to our dance and you invited your father?'

'Uh-huh,' I say.

Angel bites her lip when she's thinking. She's skinny with these mad intense eyes. Teachers love her because she gets it – Chemistry, Algebra, Civics, doesn't matter. She sucks up knowledge like a little kid slurps chocolate milk. I'm the underachiever. Even when I pretend school matters it seems pointless.

My mother finished her dissertation but died before she could defend it. Now that is wasted potential. What the fuck business does death have with people like her? I have a file of questions I wanted to ask her like whether she loved anyone before Dad or if she ever tried marijuana.

'I kind of like Sylvie. Not like that, but she's smarter than Lucien,' Angel pulls me out of my Zen moment, twisting the silver ring she got for her fifteenth birthday.

Sure, a ferret would test better than Lucien. He's on the boy's swim team and although he's hot in a swimsuit, there isn't much else to like. Angel moves closer to me on the bed. Then I get it; Angel, the reason I go to school at all, is in the B category of LGBTQ.

'If you're going to say what I think you're going to say, don't say it.' I stand up but the room isn't wide enough for me to pace. B is fine. Most of us are B, just not with a best friend.

'This isn't about you, Lulu.' She rolls up her sleeve and shows me tiny cuts lined up like a strange hieroglyphic. Didn't see that coming. I fumble with the zippered pocket in my fleece vest and swallow hard but there's an egg-sized lump in my throat. *#unchartedterritory*

'Got to go. Text you later,' I'm towering over her cross-legged on the bed with her sleeve still rolled up and a geometric design of scabs and lines on her left arm. She pulls her sleeve back down and stretches out her legs.

'Not a regular thing, Lu.'

The milk I have to pick up for my father becomes urgent. I am a devoted daughter and my father is a grieving man with a wedding to plan. It's the least I can do to keep our household supplied with milk until the lady with the stupid flower name moves in. Neither of us likes to clean so maybe we could give that over to Freesia.

What happens to awkward moments? I mean, I'm only fifteen but my bin is full. We used to pretend not to care. People laughed when I brought my father to the dance. Angel told me it was genius, that bringing Sylvie wasn't half as surprising as bringing my father. *#cluesforthe clueless*

Is cutting training for suicide? This is way beyond whimsy. We have the dead bro service to go to and my father's wedding in Vermont next month. Dad promised us extra days at the inn with my aunt when they take off on their honeymoon to Montreal and Quebec. *#cantputitbackinthebox*

'It's a mood thing. You know how I get about the dead bro service. Stressfest.' Angel swings her legs over the side of the bed.

'Sure,' I say because we've now made an agreement to have this sack of tension between us. I'll haul it to Vermont and plunk it in front of me at the wedding.

The thing about consorts in whimsy is that sometimes they do what the fuck they want, even if it pokes a hole right through the other person. I close the door and pass Angel's mother on the stairs. She gives me a big smile because I'm the perfect friend for her daughter.

'Do you want to ride with us to the service?'

'Sorry. I promised I'd go with my father and his fiancée.'

A lie told with an earnest face is always believed. Freesia said she thought it was ridiculous to have a public church service for a stillborn baby all these years later. This wasn't just any service. There would be prayers and testimonials and a reception that uses up the better part of an afternoon. Angel's mother beams at me because I'm lucky enough to have a father who finally got over his wife dying.

My mother was a grown woman with a career and most of a Ph.D. finished. If anyone was trying to make the community better, it was my mother. Your son never had a chance to make memories with your family so it's not the same. It's not anywhere near the same.

Maybe I close the door hard enough for Angel to hear. I know she's standing at the top of the stairs. In about five minutes, she'll text me a joke or one of our hashtags like *#viciouslabradoodles* or *#kittensforacause*. The secret club of us except there's a folded-over corner and that sack of tension.

I don't know why she doesn't sell her phones on eBay, even for cheap. There are people out there who need to get in touch with someone. It's selfish to hoard something that could benefit others.

Maybe there wouldn't be an Angel if Bryant didn't die. Who knows what goes through the brains of parents when they decide to have children? I buy a gallon of milk even though we only need a quart. I hope Freesia likes milkshakes and lattes. Dad said I could move to the guestroom so the two of them could have the whole upstairs. I'll have my own bathroom and a little deck. On summer mornings I can eat breakfast out there.

Dad isn't home so I Google 'cutting' before I hear the text.

Awks. Sorry. Then she calls.

'I'm donating my phones to this organisation that reconditions them and gives them away.'

'Good,' I say, doodling on the note my father left about the weekend and the long hours he'd be out with Freesia. I can paint the room any colour I want and buy some deck furniture.

'Your mother loved eating breakfast out there. It gets the morning sun,' he told me.

'La La Land,' Angel says.

'Pastel dresses,' I say. 'Matchbox cars. Jazz music.'

Saturday is a day we usually spend together even though the dead bro ceremony is on Sunday.

'Fake, Lulu. Did it with a paperclip and a red Sharpie.' *#notacutter*

I think about the crisscrossed lines on her arm and I'm pretty sure some of them looked deep enough to draw blood. The site said it might be self-soothing or a way of coping with stress.

'Got me,' I say.

Angel's roar of a laugh fills my ear. She'll buy chips and I'll download some jazz on my phone. I tell her about the room downstairs and the little deck. I'm thinking of painting it burgundy or a dark yellow.

'Ketchup and mustard,' Angel says. 'All you need are burgers, a grill and a potted freesia.'

Endgame

Nadia, why did you run off with Teller? Your mother will never recover. She dusts your picture every day and checks her phone obsessively. Teller wanted to control you; we could see it. Maybe initially you felt relief in not making decisions but as you now know, it was temporary. One day he told you not to sing or to wear the blouse instead of the t-shirt and you realised you were losing yourself. I remember the songs you made up and then the ones you sang from grade school stages and finally an auditorium. You're young enough to enter another flight plan. I can't bear to see your mother so diminished by your absence. She gets up every night and scribbles in her journal, memories of your childhood and our holidays at Bluff Point. You'd hardly recognise her.

'Declan, what are you doing up at this hour?' Constance-not-Connie is wearing a bathrobe the colour of cabernet. Her hair is frizzed around her head like a rain cloud.

'Couldn't sleep. Going out for a drive.' I close my notebook, slip the silver pen in my pocket.

'It's four in the morning!'

'I want to watch the sunrise.'

'I'm going back to bed.' She pads back to our queen-sized bed with the cotton sheets and wedding ring quilt her great grandmother made. I had it restored for our twenty-fifth anniversary, not because I like it but because she is attached to all reminders of the woman who read her Shakespeare as well as the *Bible*. She will pull the quilt around her as she does every night, even in the summer when the heat makes me sleep on top. Sleep is like death. We spend seven or eight hours unconscious. Having a spouse nearby doesn't make us less alone. Our bodies are a personal prison and the world is the larger cage.

I make my living attempting to be one step ahead of cybercriminals who exist to destroy the lives of people they don't know. I still think about the mountains at dusk, sunrise over the Atlantic and a red fox spied from my car on the way to work. I hope a better angel comes down to earth and sucks up all the corruption and greed, nothing less. We're meant to learn something in this lifetime and I'm trying. My lesson thus far is this: we are prey. Constance-not-Connie tells me to live in the moment. Good advice except life is both created and destroyed in moments. Shiva knew this. The Doomsday Clock grows ever closer to the end.

In my line of work I see the worst of humanity; foreign hackers trying to influence an election, technology wizards crippling corporate and government websites. It isn't always possible to find the motives. Sometimes when I do, it is simply power. Last week I foiled an attempt to steal client information from a local Department of Health database. It's Sunday and today I have a more important job to do.

It is in my character to be a fatalist just as it is in my wife's to nurture. I don't begrudge her that, Constance-not-Connie. I married her for it, trusting like a pair of too tight socks she would leave an impression. Marriage is the hope that love can alleviate our loneliness. For Connie, the tragedy has a face: Nadia. Nadia became an island we couldn't visit. Now Connie escapes to a classroom where she jokes and compliments, hoping that the girl in the corner with the stutter will discover Gwendolyn Brooks or Elizabeth Bishop. Like love, it is a temporary fix. She would disagree. What about the ones who rose above it all? Cheyenne Castellanos' second book of poetry comes out next year and she's invited us to the 92nd Street Y to hear her read. Cheyenne of the one-room flat, crackers and Kool-Aid for lunch. Cheyenne who cared for her younger brothers while her mother worked all day as an aide and bartended at night.

I never talk to her about Nadia. As a child Nadia would come to me, afraid of disappointing her mother. We'd talk over Sunday breakfast while Connie was at church, praying to a God neither of us believed would save us. Connie's need to make atrocity into redemption allows her to drag herself out of bed, even on the days when ice pellets bounce off the roof.

It's a weekend but that doesn't matter. Same length of time and similar fate. I won't have to make excuses for my jeans because the office isn't open, though in time zones all around the world criminals are clicking keys and upending governments and commerce. I consider it a metaphor of the times. Some of the attacks are quite ingenious, a trove of information exposing corruption at the deepest levels. My job is to protect vital infrastructure though I'm often distracted by complex codes and computer worms. The hackers are our Beelzebub, in basements and offices, planning bloodless coups. I don't understand the impetus though I suspect it is usually that old God, money.

Mervin nuzzles my hand, thinking that perhaps it isn't such an outlandish time for a walk. My moments of peace often come from walking with him, watching his pointed nose sniff the morning air, his eyes track a fly or raven. Mervin doesn't contemplate life or death. His enjoyment of kibble or a treat I carry in my pocket is unabashed. His tail wags, his tongue lolls and he bounds up to me as if I matter. I know I'm projecting onto the relationship but that is why we have pets. They ask little of us, unlike children. They'll never blame us for our shortcomings or hide when we come home.

I don't feel the cold even though I can see my breath when I walk to the car. No one is up. Even the animals seem silent except for a faint creaking that may be the wind through tree branches. There is somewhere I need to be and I've thought about the best way to get there. Maps and the GPS will help. The office isn't expecting me back for a couple of days. They think I've taken Connie away but she would not choose this location. I check the letter to make sure I've read it right.

Papi,
Please don't tell Mother. I need to leave Teller but I'm scared. I'll be at the Dunkin Donuts on Concord Street in Peterborough on Sunday the 25th at nine in the morning. He has guns. I've been going to church so he'll think that's where I am and hopefully won't follow me. Remember, don't tell M.
Love, N

We fooled ourselves into thinking Nadia was safely ensconced in her Master's program at The New England Conservatory. When she wasn't available for holidays, it was because of her performance schedule. Teller worked nearby at a coffee shop Nadia frequented on her way to practice. I've only met him once but he is strikingly handsome with intelligent eyes and long black hair tied up in a man bun. I don't even know his last name. I dismissed it as one of her many infatuations until she informed us that she was taking a leave from school to travel with him. His grandmother had left him some money and they wanted to go abroad. Connie fretted about it but we both decided that it wasn't the worst thing. After all, travel is also an education. They would go to Greece and Turkey where he supposedly had relatives. We heard nothing from her the entire month except one postcard of domed houses on the island of Santorini.

It's beautiful here. Teller says the white and blue symbolise the sky and sea.

When she returned, school seemed as remote as a Greek Island. They moved and didn't give us an address. In a furtive call she told us she was working in retail. The next call was from a co-worker's phone because Teller tracked her calls and messages. We received one letter postmarked Manchester, New Hampshire.

Sorry for everything. I wish things were different but I made a choice and I have to see it through.

I flip on public radio when I cross into New Hampshire. The sun is rising and it's the kind of sunrise that unfolds one colour at a time. The cooler colours blend at the horizon until the sun reveals its fire with buttery yellow and crimson. Bombs bursting in air, that strange line in the National Anthem. Destruction. The world is exploding and all I want is to hold Nadia in my arms and tell her that her Papi is here and everything will be ok. I don't know if I can protect her anymore.

Teller has guns.

It's been eight months since I've seen her. I've read obsessively about physical and psychological abuse and brainwashing. I know not to pressure her. I've brought along a familiar object. I've also loaded her favourite music onto my phone as if I'd suddenly adopted hopefulness as a pet. Connie would be proud of this bit of optimism.

No doubt Nadia contacted me because I anticipate disaster. Doing everything right is no guarantee of anything. All parents say things they regret or impose consequences that seem trivial until their child recounts them to a therapist twenty years later. Why did I want to love this much? It's a wound that still oozes. My drive-through coffee tastes bitter. I have homemade muffins, hardboiled eggs and an array of fruit in a cooler. Nadia may be hungry and we can't risk stopping anywhere. I wear a hat and sunglasses.

The town is picture postcard New England with colonials, Cape Cods and old churches and Mt Monadnock presiding over it all like a benevolent God. I had reread *Our Town*, set in Peterborough, planned a stop at Parker and Son's Coffee Roasters recommended for the best local coffee on Trip Advisor, and looked through photographs of possible hikes even though I suspected there would be no time. Ahead of me is the telltale pink and orange Dunkin Donuts sign but just as I pull into the parking lot, Nadia bangs on the back door and I press the button to unlock it.

'Go. Just go. Fast. He knows I'm not at church.'

It isn't until we're speeding on I–93 that she jumps into the front seat and I get a look at her. She's skinny with long hair and she's wearing too much makeup.

'I don't have anything with me, Papi. Not even a phone. A phone is like a GPS you know.'

Yes, I know. I make my living by knowing enough to make anyone paranoid. She knew I'd be the right one to contact.

I hand her a pay-as-you-go phone that I picked up at Target yesterday.

'Do you want to call anyone? No one will have this number.'

She stares at it as if it is alive and the tears start to flow. I open the glove box to reveal years of napkins I've stashed there and she grabs a wad. Then she calls 911, gives a description, licence plate and phone number.

'No, this is an anonymous call. He is armed and dangerous. Yes. A Blue Volkswagen Jetta. Teller Reis. R-e-i-s. That's right.'

We're in Massachusetts now and I ask her if she wants to stop. I've retrieved the cooler from the backseat and she's eaten two muffins and an apple.

'No. No stopping.' She gulps from the water bottle and reaches for a hardboiled egg.

We don't hear about the shootout until we're twenty minutes from the state line. I flip on the radio to get a weather update since clouds overhead have thickened.

Six people killed in a shootout at a diner in Peterborough, New Hampshire. Two police officers have been identified among the dead. The suspect has also been killed.

Eat or be eaten. Life is created and destroyed in seconds and Nadia has sidestepped this bullet. There will be others. I cannot keep her safe but in this moment, when it appears the threat has passed, the fist in my belly begins to loosen. I pull onto the shoulder of the highway and take her in my arms and I can't tell whose tears are soaking the front of my shirt. We sit there for a long time without talking and then the rain begins, first as a light drizzle and then a full-fledged deluge. Nadia opens the car door, grabs my hand and pulls. Outside we dance and scream until we're hoarse and soaked, our clothes sticking to our skin, hair plastered to our heads, distant thunder rumbling.

Malachite and Fallow

My first postcard from Nonno: a photograph of an elaborate building made entirely out of corn, the Corn Palace. After that, he'd send postcards three or four times a year. My mother would scrunch up her face as if they had a bad smell before handing them to me. I kept them in a shoebox on the top shelf of the closet, would take them out and read them over and over, putting a little red star on the towns I planned to visit. *Albuquerque, New Mexico, Cannon Beach, Oregon and Bellingham, Washington;* mountains, a big rock sticking out of the ocean and an old woman wearing a turquoise necklace. Maybe my grandfather was one of those jet-setting millionaires I read about in the grocery checkout line. *Prince William and his wife are vacationing on Martinique.* Could he be royalty? My mother didn't want to hear it. Anytime I brought him up, she made a face.

'Your nonno is like a conch shell. He washes up wherever he pleases,' she said, hacking into a loaf of bread.

Right before my twelfth birthday I received another postcard from Jackson, Wyoming, a photo of a huge arch made of antlers. My mother was pacing in her orange polka dot panties and electric pink bra, saying words out loud to find the perfect one for her new poem. When it was just the two of us she mostly walked around in a bra and panties. I wrapped myself in a sweatshirt and listened to Justin Timberlake through ear buds. When I waved the postcard at her, she frowned.

'Oh, so now he's in Wyoming. Ask him how he broke your grandmother's heart.'

Star Wickham, my mother, worked part time for the art centre but mostly she looked after me and wrote poetry that was published in magazines. She was younger and prettier than all the other mothers at school. Our place was small, a rainbow Mexican blanket draped across the back of the sofa she had pushed up against the wood panelled walls. At night my mother would open up the futon for me and we'd snuggle together reading stories like *Charlie and the Chocolate Factory*. She didn't like visitors so our place stayed quiet most of the time.

'What did he do?' I asked.

'He'd disappear for months. Your nonna was depressed all the time. She only went with him once. You would have liked her. She knitted wool hats and sweaters for the shelter and she sang Irish songs to us.'

My Uncle Leif lived in Hawaii and I don't remember him. My mother said I had little cousins with hippie names, Zephyr and Hyacinth. Leif was her younger brother and supposedly we met a long time ago because we lived with Nonno, Nonna and Leif until I was two. All I remember is a clawfoot bathtub and wind chimes.

'I named you Joanna so you'd have a solid name. It's the name of a woman who can make her own way in the world.'

Leif and Zephyr sounded ok to me but I agreed about Hyacinth. Having a white toast name meant I had to work extra hard to add colour. Maybe that's why I wanted to be an artist.

Ten o'clock one Friday night, there was a knock on our door.

'Who is it?' My mother pulled aside the burlap piece covering the pane of glass and leaned against it so she could hear.

'Moi. Ton père.'

'Shit. C'mon. What's with you? You disappear for years and now you show up. It's ten o'clock for God's sake.'

My mother grabbed what she called her emergency attire from the hook in the hall closet. She opened the door and a tall grey-haired man stepped in, carrying a paper bag. He placed a six-pack in the fridge and handed me a package of Twizzlers.

'We don't eat that crap, y'know,' my mother said.

'Then you're truly missing out. Twizzlers aren't just any candy. They have flavour and texture. Best anti-smoking device I know.' Nonno ripped open the package and grabbed one with his forefinger and middle finger like a cigarette.

'Try it, Joanie.'

I was sitting cross-legged in my mallard duck pajamas, with the Harry Potter book still open.

'Your grandfather.' My mother made a gesture like she was formally introducing him.

'Pleased to make your acquaintance, Mademoiselle Joanie.' Nonno stuck out his hand and I shook it.

He stayed about two hours, drank three beers and ate a cheese sandwich with Dijon mustard and avocado.

'Why Provincetown?'

'The art and the sea,' my mother said.

'Is it the best place for the child?' He sipped from the can of beer, took a bite of the sandwich.

'You know, she's right here. She's not invisible or deaf or anything.'

'I like it here,' I said. 'We go out on the boat to study marine science sometimes and I have friends.'

After Nonno left, my mother locked the door and pulled the curtains. It was after midnight and I had dozed off on the futon even though I heard their voices all jumbled together like a summer night walking down Commercial Street. *Betterschoolsirresponsiblecontemporaryartherfuturemisunderstandingimsorryapostcardtakecarenow.* There was a soft whisper when my mother closed the door and the wind moved across the room, stirring up a magazine and the pages of the Harry Potter book. I pulled the thick blanket up to my chin and I heard my mother open the closet to hang her emergency attire back on its hook.

The next day I was lounging in the bathtub, running bubble bath under the spout when my mother knocked on the door.

'I don't want you to be fooled by him, Joanie.'

'What do you mean?'

'He's a storyteller. My mother would wait for him to call. Sometimes we didn't hear from him for weeks.'

'You mean he lies?'

'Joanie-bear, his stories are to lies what a tsunami is to a wave. A professional. Once they left me with a neighbour for three weeks so my mama could go with him on one of his business trips. Awful for both of us.'

Our next-door neighbours, Pete and Oliver, seemed nice enough but I don't think my mother would have left me with them.

'Why did you make him a sandwich?' I asked.

'He is my father. A sandwich I can do. Letting him take you on a trip is a different story. Promise me you'll be careful.'

Did he ask to take me on a trip? I tried to remember what I heard before I fell asleep. I had more questions but my mother closed the door.

Nonno didn't show up again for six years, three weeks before my high school graduation. I had dyed my hair green with a streak of pink to celebrate.

'Brown hair is so mac and cheese,' I told my mother.

She laughed, 'My father once challenged me to come up with the strangest colours – you know, like vermillion or chartreuse. Your hair is peppermint stick.'

'How about magenta and azure?' I said.

'You're good at this game; sign of a creative mind.'

I talked her into buying me a turquoise kimono with a yellow sash for the class party. I was remaking myself, beginning with graduation. I know she thought naming me Joanie would make me conventional but I was probably more of a Zephyr.

I didn't tell her about the call from Nonno, how we'd arranged to get together that afternoon.

Nonno took a ferry from Boston and I met him at MacMillan Wharf.

'Wow, You look like an ice-cream sundae with a fresh-picked cherry on top!' He smelled like cedar and orange peel when he grabbed me in a hug.

We went out for coffee and he poured lots of cream in his. Coffee was a newly-acquired taste for me so I loaded it down with honey and milk. Nonno gave me a surprisingly-large check for graduation. The card was a cartoon he drew himself, a girl with curly hair and a mortarboard hat flying down a mountain on skies.

'You're skiing into the rest of your life. You'd be doing me a favour if you don't tell your mother about this,' he sipped his creamy coffee, wiped off his milk moustache.

I wasn't sure if he meant the meeting or the money or both.

'Can't change the past, Joanna, but I'm betting life has some surprises in store for you.'

When I walked him back to the ferry he moved slowly, so I tried to pace my steps to his.

'I'll send you a postcard,' he said.

Years later, when I was a new college graduate, Nonno invited me to dinner. We agreed to meet at a restaurant near my apartment. White-haired, tall and thin, he cut an imposing figure, even with a cane.

'Do you ever think about the hundreds of other people that sat in this booth before us; couples breaking up relationships, people falling in love? We're part of something way bigger, don't you think?' Then he took a breath and a gulp of water. 'How's your mama?'

'Ok,' I said. 'Misses me.'

'I'll bet,' he put his hand on his chin. 'If she hadn't gotten pregnant so young she probably would have gone to graduate school and become a professor. We were wrong to try to talk her out of it though. She did a good job with you.'

They tried to talk her out of having me?

The old woodwork and chandelier gave the restaurant a feel of elegance. I had already glanced at the menu, reminding myself that he asked me out. This wasn't a place I could afford.

'Figured it was time for us to meet again before I shove off to parts unknown. Big sky or maybe the deep sea.' Nonno twirled his Hulk Hogan style moustache. 'Nice rainbow streak in your hair. How'd you like art school?'

'The best. Mom didn't think it was practical but she's a poet. Guess I'm doomed to be poor. How do you get by when you move so much?' I asked.

'Place is here,' Nonno tapped his chest. 'Everything else is a slice of melon or a sprig of parsley, just garnish. You can live near the coast or in the heartland with rolling fields and more cows than people. What does it matter? I have friends all over the country, made my own way.'

'What about family?'

Nonno took another gulp of water.

'Your momma left home at eighteen. Your uncle stayed until he was almost twenty-five. Now he's in Hawaii and she's in Provincetown and I have only me to look out for. Keeping an eye on you though.'

'I'm ok.'

He patted his moustache again with the napkin. 'Not so easy to travel now that I'm older. Besides, airport security is a bitch, doncha think? I got this metal piece in my arm and it sets off the detectors. Some agent comes to grope me. Ever been groped by airport security?'

I shook my head. I had only flown once.

'Sooner or later everyone's luck runs out. Not all starfish and surfers on the beach. Did you ever get a bad sunburn, the kind where your skin blisters and it hurts to put on a shirt?'

I nodded.

'Got knees that hurt all the time. Bone rubbing on bone, feels like. Worse than sunburn,' he said.

'That's awful. Can't you get a shot or something?'

'Sure I can. Just saying that you've got to take the bad with the good. Maybe you won't take as long as I did to learn that. And don't hold grudges. I'd give anything to make peace with your Mama.'

'What did you do to get her so mad?'

'When you're trying to make your mark, it takes time. I thought I was doing the right thing but life is short, Joanna. Don't be a jackass and stay close to people you love,' he said. 'Don't judge. None of us are mind-readers, if you know what I mean.'

I didn't. 'What do you mean?'

'Used to lose my temper and I had my own ideas of right and wrong. Before I knew it, your Nonna was gone and your mother wouldn't talk to me. I was too hard on her and it wasn't her fault.'

'What wasn't?'

'Wish I could go back in time. When we left your mama and Leif with the neighbours for three weeks, their son bothered your mama. My fault. Leif even said he didn't want to stay there. We don't get a redo, Joanna. Got to get it right the first time.'

'Mom told me you left her and Leif with a neighbour but I didn't know the rest.' I said. 'Like he abused her?' I touched the phone in my pocket, thought of ducking into the ladies room to call my mother. My mother only went on one date that I remember. She slammed the door and took a shower as soon as she got home. When I asked her she said he only invited her to the exhibit as an excuse to get her into bed.

'I'm not saying all men are like this but a woman has to be prepared and always have a Plan B, like a ride or a phone to call someone,' she told me.

Nonno hesitated. 'Your mama should be the one to tell you this but you're an adult now and you have a right to know. First we heard it from Leif but then it became obvious. When she had you, she seemed happy again,' he said, popping a pill from a plastic container.

'The neighbour kid got her pregnant? I'm the product of a rape?' I felt nauseous, tightened my grip on my phone.

Nonno's eyes seemed fixed on his napkin and he sipped some more water, ran his fingers through his hair. He looked distinguished in an old man kind of way.

'She didn't want to press charges and she wanted to have you. Neighbour kid said it was consensual but the family shipped him out of town pretty fast. A year later the rest of the family moved away.' Nonno fixed his eyes on me.

'Got any photos of your paintings?'

I knew he was deliberately changing the subject and I needed time in my head to rewrite a significant part of my life story. I pulled up my Instagram; fragments of boats, sun bouncing off water, a spaghetti box and copies of the comic strip *Half Sour Pickle* I drew for the college newspaper.

'What's that one?' He pointed to my copy of Blue Nude II.

'A copy of a Matisse I did for an art class. Had it hanging in our apartment for a while.'

'Wow. I wouldn't know that from a real Matisse.'

I don't know if he ever saw a real Matisse but I flushed with pride.

'Did you really go to all those places in the postcards?' I asked him.

'Yes indeed. That was the best part, meeting people from all over, seeing this beautiful country. It's easy to think where you live is all there is but some people in other places talk with an accent, eat interesting food and even dress differently. It made me more aware.'

'Where are you going next?' I asked.

'Arizona. Need some sunshine. Remember, we share blood. Nothing will change that,' he said. 'You will always be in here.' He put his hand over his heart.

I held onto his elbow as I walked him into the train station. He only had a leather briefcase.

'Where's your luggage?'

'I like to travel light,' he said.

If I could have stepped out of my life and gotten on that train I would have.

'I'll send you a postcard when I get there. Your artwork is good but you have to sell yourself, Joanna. Everyone wants a world with more beauty, don't they?'

'I guess.' I kissed him on the cheek.

Three weeks later I got a streaky pink sky and saguaro cactus postcard from the Painted Desert in Arizona. The back said: *Dr Ian Wickham died on November 2. I am his lawyer and friend. Please contact me.* There was an address and phone number. I don't know why I called the number before I called my mother. Dr Ian Wickham? Doctor of what? My heart literally ached.

We were requested to appear in Arizona for the reading of his will.

'Nonno was a doctor?' I called her later than usual and she picked up on the first ring.

'He worked as a professor before he gave it up. Never wanted anyone to know because he thought professors were snobs but probably there is more to that story,' she said.

'Nonno told me about the neighbour.'

A long pause.

'I guess I should thank you for having me. I sure wasn't that brave at seventeen,' I said.

Finally she spoke. 'Nonna helped. You probably don't remember her but she'd wake up with you at night so I could get up for school the next day. Because of her I finished high school and went to college.'

'Didn't Nonno help?'

'Paid the bills, I guess. He travelled most of the time. He shouldn't have left us. Leif couldn't stand those neighbours.'

'We have to go to Arizona to hear about the will.' I said.

'You know I hate to travel. Why don't you represent both of us? I'm sure he doesn't have much. He sold the house years ago. Probably just artwork and personal stuff.'

I wanted her to sob over the phone but she sounded strangely calm. I was the one choking over my words and blowing my nose. I spent the evening going through my two shoeboxes of postcards: my grandfather's life.

Palm trees and cactus and a dizzying array of flowers decorated the lawn of a large stucco house.

A short man with glasses greeted me at the door, offered his hand.

'Bob Friedman,' he said. 'Have a seat, Ms Wickham.' I sat in a plump leather chair the colour of a ripe plum.

'Dr Wickham liked to keep his business private.'

He pulled out a stack of paper held together with a binder clip. 'Here are the locations of the six *Malachite and Fallow* galleries. A new one is due to open in Provincetown, Massachusetts in April.'

Jackson, Wyoming, Bellingham, Washington, Cannon Beach, Oregon, Albuquerque, New Mexico. Postcard towns.

'*Malachite and Fallow*? What is that? Does my mother know?'

'I don't believe anyone in your family knows. Dr Wickham left explicit instructions not to tell anyone until his death. *Malachite and Fallow* are popular wine bars with attached art galleries. The concept caught on after a bumpy start with the first one, here in Tucson. My driver can take you there after we're done. Your grandfather left the business to you with the remainder of his estate going to his children, Star and Leif. He tried to apologise to your mother. He told me you gave him a second chance.'

Bob Friedman crossed and uncrossed his legs and adjusted his wire-rimmed glasses. I asked him to tell me more about the wine bars.

'An art nouveau decor but the art ranges from comic art to impressionism. Every month, an artist is featured and there is a reception. Your grandfather travelled all over to find the artists. He felt you were suited for this since you have a background in art history. He was proud of you, Ms Wickham.'

When I walked into the gallery and wine bar, a magenta and orange turbaned young man rushed me at the door. Behind the cash register, I saw a photo of my grandparents with my mother and Leif. Next to that was a photo of me, taken at my high school graduation, my green and pink hair poking out of the hat.

'Joanna Wickham. Delighted to finally meet you. I loved your grandfather.'

He went on to tell me about his stint in prison for drugs and how my grandfather took a chance on him, training him to take over the gallery ten years ago.

Then I travelled to Jackson, Wyoming and saw the Antler Arches and the tiny pink and green lights around the *Malachite and Fallow* sign. A young woman with blue hair spontaneously hugged me. The same photos in different frames were on the wall behind the cash register.

'When your grandfather was in town, he gave me art books to read and bought me supplies. I was pregnant when he hired me. He made sure I didn't have to lift anything. Such a nice man.'

It wasn't until Cannon Beach, Oregon that I met someone who didn't like him.

'So you're the granddaughter. He said your mother wouldn't let him see you so he waited until you were eighteen. He told us you'd be taking over someday. This is a small community and some folks still hold a grudge because he'd hire people who didn't fit in, if you know what I mean.'

I thought of my thirty-five-year-old mother watching me get my high school diploma. No one in Provincetown cared that she was younger than the other mothers or fathers. Families look all different ways in my hometown.

I called my mother to tell her that she would need to manage the Provincetown *Malachite and Fallow* when it opened in April.

'It's in the East End. You can help with the design.'

'*Malachite and Fallow*? No kidding? When he challenged me at the colour game, I cheated and looked it up. He said the game was over because malachite and fallow were so original,' her voice cracked. 'How the hell did he have a chain of galleries or whatever without us knowing? Why did he plan one in Provincetown without telling me?'

I couldn't answer her questions.

'You could give a break to those musicians outside the town hall trying to make it from the coins people throw in a guitar case,' I said.

'What if they're on drugs?' she said. Her voice squeaked. 'You know he travelled all the time and didn't give a hoot when he left us with those crazy neighbours.'

Maybe Nonno thought his travelling was a price of being a successful man.

'He wanted to make things right with you,' I said.

'I know. He called me a few times but I wasn't ready.' Her voice broke up.

'You're going to have to get some clothes for your new job. The bra and panties won't work,' I said.

She laughed. 'Ok, Joanie. I get it.'

I sent my mother a postcard from Bellingham, Washington; invited her to visit. The Pacific Ocean is different from the Atlantic, I told her. I'm thinking of setting up poetry readings in the galleries. *I want you to be our first reader.*

Second Lives

When I slip the tiny bird whistle into my carryon bag, Sylvan spots it.

'If my father's Purple Heart and signet ring can't go with us, neither can your stupid whistle. We're starting fresh, Beth.'

I sneak the whistle into my pocket in the bathroom. It comforts me on days when I'm afraid to answer the door. Sylvan says I need medication, one of those drugs that quiet voices, even though I know Aunt Vicky is telling me about the trails in Keelen Forest, behind the gas station. Sometimes I see a wild turkey or a doe nibbling at dry grass. Since they built the rails-to-trails, there's no worry of poison ivy or ticks. There's something about wildness I love. Sylvan thinks I'm at a yoga class or drinking coffee with friends I don't have. Aunt Vicky said he has bad karma and that the universe will teach him a lesson. After the accident she said he'd be haunted the rest of his life and there wasn't any escaping it.

My backpack has this tiny compartment for glasses or maybe a passport. I could put the whistle there. It's not a weapon or one of the items you can't bring on a plane so I won't need to put it in the plastic bin. When Sylvan takes his shower I zip it into the tiny pouch. My body relaxes because I know when I land in Ireland there will be one thing friendly and familiar.

I used to think Sylvan and I were best friends because we'd been through near-death. When they stitched him back together, I thought he'd become more real like the Velveteen Rabbit. Instead the scars looked like frowns all over his face and the ridges on his hands were hard and angry. My scar runs up my left ankle but no one sees it since I wear pants. We had a little house once, a dormered Cape down the street from the city park. The lawyers took it away, told us that everything Sylvan made from here on out would go to the family of the boy who died.

Sylvan said, 'What's the point of working?' Sylvan said, 'We need to blow this place sky high.' Sylvan said, 'Let's go to Ireland.' Aunt Vicky said he couldn't run away from his responsibilities and the authorities wouldn't allow it. I didn't say much, just played with my whistle and walked on the trails while Sylvan went to the office to make money to give away. I knew it was his fault but he's been paying and paying and he says there's no more money. Sylvan said, 'We may as well just live on the street with the amount they let us keep each month.' Now we live in a one-room apartment with a miniature stove and tiny refrigerator in a not-so-great neighbourhood. There's a dumpster outside so we can't even open the window on hot days.

When I tried to get a job, Sylvan told me I wasn't employable.

'You don't understand things.'

I applied anyway – at a daycare, an insurance company in a grey office building and at the Last Stop Diner. When the diner called me back, I didn't answer the phone because we'd already decided to use the passports we got three years ago for our trip to Montreal. On a Saturday we drove up to the border station and they asked questions like *how long are you staying* and *what is your business in Canada?* Sylvan told them we were on our honeymoon, which was a half-truth, not a full-blown lie. We had a pretend wedding when we bought the Cape, saying vows we wrote:

'I will cook you lasagne with extra cheese on top.'

'All dinners will be by candlelight.'

Sylvan promised not to go looking for me when I disappeared for a few hours as long as I came back before dark. I could tell this was hard for him because he curled his lip and showed his teeth like a German shepherd once did when I crossed her path on the trail. Sylvan gave me a silver ring with a light green stone and a forest green dress with smocking. I hadn't talked to my mother in two years but I left her a message that I'd gotten married. 'His name is Sylvan. He sells insurance'. She didn't call back but I'm sure she told Lyndon. Sylvan said brothers are supposed to be protective of their little sisters but Lyndon called me *Scrawny* and *Dumbass.* He might live somewhere near a coast or he might not. Maybe he died in a shark attack or an earthquake.

I take out my whistle and think of Aunt Vicky who lived with Aunt Earla all her life. They went to Las Vegas every year and I had Vegas names for them, *Violet* and *Bunny*. I gave them a wardrobe they kept in storage, feather boas and sequined dresses. It's important to have a second life when your first one isn't going so well.

Aunt Vicky had listened with her whole face turned toward me like the rest of the room was a blur and I was in focus. She made popcorn in a cast-iron pot and poured melted butter over it. We'd eat fistfuls or put it in paper bags and take with us on a walk. Whatever was left, we'd scatter for the birds or ducks by the little pond in the back of her apartment. Sylvan said she wasn't a real aunt because she was my stepfather's sister. She didn't mind if my hair was sticking up or I forgot the name of a cross street. Aunt Vicky gave me the whistle and a box that said *Bethany* in gold block letters. She also took me to see *Hairspray.* Even though I had met Sylvan by then, she didn't invite him because she said, 'Wednesday will be our day, Bethany. We'll dress up and take the train.' I wore my forest green dress and Aunt Vicky wore hot pink slacks with matching ballet flats. She bought me a giant pretzel from a one-eyed man with a rolling cart, showed me how to squirt mustard on it, but she didn't tell me about her heart. Sylvan said that some people don't like others to feel sorry for them so they keep their troubles a secret. Aunt Earla died a month after Aunt Vicky. Sylvan said that maybe they couldn't live without each other. I still have her number stored in my phone but when I call it a voice says it's not a working number.

My sister used to call me Breathany because I have asthma and sometimes it's hard to catch my breath. I don't know what she calls me now because we don't talk anymore. Sylvan said families are how we get here and then it's up to us to make a life for ourselves. He said his story is mixed up with my story because we have *destiny.* I wish I had lived with Aunt Vicky so we could have walked on the Freedom Trail. We never finished all the hikes we circled in red on the map but we did sixteen of them, including one a couple of weeks ago where we had to stop because Aunt Vicky was weak and couldn't walk anymore. I bought a yellow highlighter and coloured over the ones we finished and I drew a sad face on the one we didn't finish. We made up our own names for them – *Dirty Puddle Trail, McDonald's Litter Trail, Flat Rock Path.* My favourite was *Stinkhorn Trail* where a row of the mushrooms looked like Army guys in front of the recruiting station. Aunt Vicky said stinkhorns smelled bad if you stepped on them but they were the colour of a sunrise. We took something from every trail and gave something back. 'It's a way of respecting nature,' Aunt Vicky had told me. In my Bethany box, I have flat rocks, dried stalks, pressed flowers and leaves and a stick shaped like a slingshot. We gave back seeds we carried in our pockets, crumbs, popcorn for the birds or animals, or water from a big bottle we brought if it was one of those seasons without enough rain.

Sylvan bought our plane tickets and I put mine in the Bethany box next to my passport. He gave our dishes to Gillian and Arthur who live next door, told them they could have our pots and pans and toaster too. The rest he carried to the dumpster, old boots and a plastic salad spinner. We took the mugs with faces on them and forks and spoons. Sylvan went to the library to find a place to rent in a town called Shannon, near the airport. He had about two thousand dollars that he had saved before the lawyers took everything from his bank accounts. He kept it in a metal box with a lock on it and he wouldn't even show me where he hid the key. Aunt Vicky's money was in a money belt under my t-shirt.

'This will be enough to start over if you need it. Don't forget to leave something and take something.' When I asked her about Las Vegas, she told me about Billy Cronin and Mitch Mitchell, the blackjack table and chocolate martinis rimmed with powdered sugar.

'We were silly women, Bethie. Silly, silly women.' When they won the jackpot, Aunt Vicky already knew about her heart disease.

'You can't buy time, Bethie but you can buy chances.'

I picked a town called Tralee because it sounded like a song. They have a Rose of Tralee Festival. It's eighty-one miles from Shannon Airport but they use kilometres in Ireland. There's a harbour and boats and it's in a county called Kerry. My rental is on Wild Atlantic Way and I tell Aunt Vicky about it even though she can't hear me anymore. From the pictures I saw on the library computer, I'll be able to see the ocean from the kitchen table.

Sylvan said we're definitely staying in Shannon because it's convenient and near the airport. Because we're only pretend married, my bank accounts aren't mixed up with his and Aunt Vicky told me not to share about the money.

'A woman needs to be independent, Bethie.'

When we deposited her winnings, I got a blue plastic card with my name on it so I could take out money when I wanted a pair of shoes or a grilled cheese. She showed me how to use an ATM machine with a password I picked because it was her birthday. I pat the wad of cash next to my stomach. Flying was like being in another world, Aunt Vicky told me, kind of like that time we laid on our backs on the moss and looked up at a sky so bright it made my eyes water.

We didn't have a car anymore so Sylvan took the bus to work. It stopped down the street and smelled like diesel fuel. He carried a little cloth briefcase stuffed with papers and his laptop, wore a grey suit or blue suit with a yellow shirt or white shirt every day except Saturday and Sunday. Sylvan said he liked selling insurance because he was helping people pretend they could protect their future. Sylvan said it didn't work out for us. Sylvan said insurance is for fools who think that companies are going to pay when something bad happens. He had car insurance but not the million-dollar kind, just the kind most people get. Sylvan said life insurance only pays out when you're dead so what's the use of that? Aunt Vicky had life insurance and now it's in a trust that I can have whenever I want it. Because of Vegas I don't need it. Sylvan said that Aunt Vicky was dumb about money because she rented instead of buying and the rent kept going up.

The ring he gave me was a peridot set in silver, not an emerald set in gold. Aunt Vicky told me that was a sign of how cheap he was, that he wouldn't even spring for a precious stone set in gold even though he had money then. I liked it anyway because green beams bounced off the walls when I was washing dishes.

When the policemen came to the door I was in the bathroom adjusting my money belt.

'What you say can be used against you in a court of law.'

From the bathroom window I saw the officers putting Sylvan in the back seat of the police car. Sylvan wasn't supposed to go out of the country.

Sylvan said, 'Those fuckers can't make me stay here and give everything to the dead kid's family.'

Aunt Vicky said you can add to the problems of the world or you can subtract from them. She said Sylvan did something very wrong. I was holding her hand and the room smelled like Lysol and balsam from the two sachets I put by her bed so she could pretend she was in the forest.

Before my cab pulls up, I move the whistle to my pocket though I know I'll have to put it in the plastic bin. Aunt Vicky told me about taking off my shoes and belt and walking through a door with x-rays that can see if I've hidden anything. Money is ok because it doesn't set off the alarms. I leave my phone on the table along with the rent. Our landlord has kids and they need sneakers and lunch money. My phone vibrates. When it quiets I delete everything like Sylvan showed me.

I don't know much about the law but I do know that red lights are for stopping and the children matter maybe more than adults because they have years ahead of them. I don't think I'll have one. Aunt Vicky lost a child once. She was engaged to the father but she broke it off when the baby got born before it was even a baby. Aunt Earla told her it was nature's way. Aunt Vicky said she cried so many tears she needed a bath towel to sop them up. Then she had no more tears and went to Las Vegas to play blackjack and watch the performers in their sparkling suits and gowns.

'But you'll have a dear baby one day, Bethie. A dear, dear baby that you'll sing to and love.'

In my second life, I will wear a wool sweater and call it a jumper. I'll learn to drive because I'm careful and obey signs and lights. Aunt Vicky said that Sylvan was an angry man who didn't like women. Sylvan said Aunt Vicky needed to get laid but I think Aunt Vicky was ok just dreaming about Mitch Mitchell and Billy Cronin. She didn't want another baby to grow inside her.

The cab isn't yellow but blue. Gillian and Arthur are at the window watching the driver lift my luggage into the trunk. The cab driver wears a hat so I know he's a real driver.

'Which airline, Miss?'

We pull in behind the other cabs and shuttles and I pay him out of the money I put in my pocket. A family pushes ahead of me in line, children with small rolling bags. They are laughing, one cuddling a stuffed rabbit and the other holding a Lego truck.

My seat by the window was supposed to be for Sylvan. I push my backpack under the seat in front of me. There is no one next to me because Sylvan is in a holding cell somewhere, or at least that's what they do on television when they catch the criminal. They called his name three times over a loudspeaker. I look out the little window with its pull-down plastic shade. Two men and a woman are loading the luggage into the bottom of the plane. It's a dirty day, the kind Aunt Vicky called dismal. The sky looks like a puddle. I hope it doesn't rain because I want to see us lift up into the sky. There are clanks before they announce: *Flight attendants prepare for takeoff. Please make sure your seatbelt is securely fastened and your personal items are stowed beneath the seat in front of you.*

I watch the lifejacket and oxygen mask demonstrations as the engines roar and we roll down the runway. People and trucks begin to look smaller and smaller until I can't see them at all and then the clouds and puddle of sky disappear and there's nothing but blue – dish detergent blue, bluebird blue. We're in the blue and it's on both sides of the plane.

I twist off the peridot ring, drop it in the little pocket with magazines and exit instructions, close my eyes. When I open them we're sailing in clouds and everything is fluffy and fresh. I order a Coke that I don't have to pay for and unwrap tinfoil chicken in a rosy sauce. It's ok to hold my bird whistle now so I get it out of my backpack and stand it on the tray table next to my dinner. On a screen in front of me a tiny plane moves along a curved orange line that ends at a green dot called Ireland.

About the Author

Lisa C. Taylor is a poet and fiction writer. She has four collections of poetry: *Talking to Trees* (2007) and *Insufficient Thanks* (2012) with Finishing Line Press. Arlen House published *The Other Side of Longing* (2011), a collaborative collection of poetry with Geraldine Mills, and *Necessary Silence* (2013). Both Lisa C. Taylor and Geraldine Mills were chosen for the Elizabeth Shanley Gerson Lecture of Irish Literature at University of Connecticut in 2011. Lisa has one previous collection of short fiction with Arlen House, *Growing a New Tail*, published in 2015.

Lisa's honours include winning the 2015 Hugo House New Works Fiction Award, nominations for the Pushcart Prize in both fiction and poetry, a Best Indie Lit nomination for fiction in 2014, and a Surdna Arts Teaching Fellowship. Lisa has been featured in interviews in *The Worcester Review* and *Sonder Review* and she was a Spotlight Feature on the Associated Writing Programs (AWP) in 2015. Her books have been taught in college classes, most recently in 2018. Lisa was a visiting writer at Norwalk Community College in the fall semester of 2017 and a mentor in the AWP Writer-to-Writer program in 2016.

Lisa C. Taylor holds a Master of Fine Arts in Creative Writing from Stonecoast/University of Southern Maine. She is a fiction editor and interviewer for Wordpeace and a book reviewer and interviewer for various magazines including *Mom Egg Review*. She also holds a Master of Arts degree from University of Connecticut. Lisa currently offers private writing classes and writing workshops in the U.S. and abroad. www.lisactaylor.com She tweets at @dreamingchange